No one else was in the dimly lit corridor. All she could hear was the sound of her heart thudding in her ears. Suddenly he dipped forward and his mouth hovered just millimetres away from hers.

Now. Kiss me now.

She closed her eyes. It was inevitable. Any minute now she would feel his lips devouring hers.

Instead his lips brushed against her ear. 'Thank you, Francesca,' he whispered. He stepped back, his breathing shallow and ragged, his eyes burning. His breathing slowed. 'Goodnight, *cara*.'

His accent stroked across her skin and she watched as his lean, athletic body turned and disappeared down the corridor.

She fell back against the door. *Wow!* Her head was spinning.

She lifted her slightly trembling hand and pushed the cabin card into the slot on her door. The door swung open and she collapsed onto the nearby bed.

He'd almost kissed her and then walked away. The sparks between them could have set the whole ship alight. She could already imagine the sensations of kissing him. A blow your mind, send you rocketing off into space, turn your legs to jelly kind of kiss. She didn't know whether to laugh, cry, or chase him along the corridor and drag him back to her room!

Everything was racing through her mind. The man she didn't want to like had nearly kissed her. And she'd let him.

Was she losing her mind?

Dear Reader

My family and I had the pleasure of cruising around the Mediterranean last year and visiting some wonderful places. It was a great experience and there was nothing like waking up in a new port every day. We visited the ruins of Pompeii and the Château D'If—the prison that inspired *The Count of Monte Cristo*.

Imagine living that life every day. The crew we met were all hardworking, dedicated professionals, and I couldn't think of a better setting for a medical romance.

Gabriel is a gorgeous Venetian doctor. He's returned home to be closer to his family as his father is unwell. He comes from a wealthy background and has a poor experience of women, who have frequently been more interested in his money than his heart.

Francesca is using the cruise ship as a safe haven while she waits for her visa to Australia. But what is she really running from?

These two had to work hard for their happy-ever-after, and I'm so glad that they get it in such a beautiful setting.

Please come and say hi at my website: www.scarlet-wilson.com

Scarlet

AN INESCAPABLE TEMPTATION

BY
SCARLET WILSON

First published in Great Britain 2013
by Mills & Boon, an imprint of Harlequin (UK) Limited.
Large Print edition 2013
Harlequin (UK) Limited, Eton House,
18-24 Paradise Road, Richmond, Surrey TW9 1SR

© Scarlet Wilson 2013

ISBN: 978 0 263 23122 9

Harlequin (UK) policy is to use papers that are natural, renewable and recyclable products and made from wood grown in sustainable forests. The logging and manufacturing process conform to the legal environmental regulations of the country of origin.

Printed and bound in Great Britain
by CPI Antony Rowe, Chippenham, Wiltshire

Scarlet Wilson wrote her first story aged eight and has never stopped. Her family have fond memories of *Shirley and the Magic Purse*, with its army of mice, all with names beginning with the letter 'M'. An avid reader, Scarlet started with every Enid Blyton book, moved on to the *Chalet School* series and many years later found Mills & Boon.

She trained and worked as a nurse and health visitor, and currently works in public health. For her, finding medical romances was a match made in heaven. She is delighted to find herself among the authors she has read for many years.

Scarlet lives on the West Coast of Scotland with her fiancé and their two sons.

Recent titles by the same author:

A BOND BETWEEN STRANGERS*
WEST WING TO MATERNITY WING!
THE BOY WHO MADE THEM LOVE AGAIN
IT STARTED WITH A PREGNANCY
**The Most Precious Bundle of All*

These books are also available in eBook format from www.millsandboon.co.uk

Dedication

My family are so lucky to have been blessed
with three beautiful babies in the last year.
Welcome to the world,
Taylor Jennifer Hyndman,
Oliver Edward Nyack, and
Noah Alexander Dickson.
Wishing you lives filled with
love, health, and happiness.

xx

CHAPTER ONE

'HELP!'

Gabriel turned his head, trying to figure out where the cry had come from amongst the bustling bodies at the port side. The Venezia Passegeri was packed—mainly with crew and harbour staff. Carts packed with passengers' luggage and an obscene amount of fresh food were being piled aboard the cruise ship in front of him, all blocking his view.

'Help! Over here. Someone help!'

The cry rippled through the crowd as heads turned and focused towards the shout. It only took Gabriel a few seconds to realise the cry was coming from the edge of the quay. He dropped his bag and pushed his way through the crowd. A woman was standing near the edge, her face pale, her breathing coming in rapid, shallow breaths. Her trembling hand was pointing towards the water.

Gabriel's eyes followed her finger. There, in the water, was a child—a teenager—struggling in the waves that already seemed to have a grip of him. He must have only just fallen in, but this part of the marina was right on the outskirts of Venice, nearest the sea, and the waves were picking him up and down as he coughed and spluttered, pulling him out to sea.

Gabriel didn't even think. He just dived in. Straight into the murky waters of Venice.

By now a few crew members had noticed the commotion and were shouting in rapid Italian. Gabriel swam quickly towards the boy. It only took a few seconds to wish he'd taken the time to remove his shoes and dress uniform jacket. They weighed him down almost instantly. His white uniform would never look the same again.

The boy kept sinking before his eyes, the waves sweeping over his head as he struggled for breath. Gabriel powered forward, anxious to reach him before he disappeared from sight again.

He got there in less than a minute but the boy had sunk under the waves. Gabriel took a deep breath and dived underwater, reaching down into the darkness. It was amazing how the strong Italian sun penetrated so little through the murky waters. Venice was renowned for its dirty canals. The cruise ship terminal was situated on the outskirts near the edge of the Adriatic Sea, where the deep-keeled ships could dock. And although the waters were marginally better here, they still looked nothing like the clear blue seas depicted in the travel brochures. His fingers brushed against something and he tried fruitlessly to grasp it. Nothing.

Frustration swept over him. His face broke the surface of the water and he gasped for air, trying to fill his lungs. Beneath the waves he shucked one foot against the other. It was a move he did every night in the comfort of his penthouse flat while sitting on the sofa, but struggling to stay afloat it was so much more awkward. Finally he felt a release as the five-hundred-euro handmade leather shoes floated down into the murky depths. Now he would find the boy.

He dived beneath the waves again, reaching out, trying to circle the area beneath him. This time he felt something bump against his hand and he grabbed tightly before kicking his burning legs to the surface. The two of them burst above the waves, the teenager's flailing legs and arms landing a panicked punch on the side of Gabriel's head.

He flinched. His brain switching into gear. The woman at the quayside had shouted in English.

'Stay still,' he hissed at the boy. The sun was temporarily blinding him as the water streamed down his face.

He could see the jetty. Figures shouted towards him but he couldn't hear a word. The current was strong here and he could hardly believe how quickly they'd moved away from the quay.

The glistening hull of the luxury cruise ship seemed so far away. He'd been standing before it only a few minutes earlier.

He put both hands around the boy's chest and pulled him backwards against his own chest, trying to swim for both of them in his version of the classic lifesaving manoeuvre.

But the boy couldn't stop panicking. The waves were fierce, the water still sweeping over the top of them, causing the boy to writhe in Gabriel's arms as he struggled for breath. A shadow loomed behind them.

His arms were aching as he fought to keep their heads above the water. How on earth was he going to get them back to the quay? Again he could hear the boy coughing and spluttering, choking on the waves that kept crashing over their heads.

He'd never done a sea rescue before. Last time he'd seen one he'd been watching TV. It had all looked so much easier then. Didn't the life-guards on TV always put people on their backs and pull them towards shore? It didn't seem to be working for him. And they had that strange red plastic thing to help them. Where were the lifebelts here? Shouldn't every port have them?

What on earth was he doing? This was mad-ness. Being a cruise ship doctor was supposed to be easy. It wasn't supposed to kill you the first day on the job.

The irony of this wasn't lost on him. He'd known this job was a bad idea right from the start. A cruise ship doctor was hardly the ideal role for a paediatrician.

But family came first.

And this had been the first job he'd been able to find at short notice. Close enough to Venice to be here when needed but far enough away not to attract any unwanted media attention.

His father's health was slowly but surely deteriorating. And the call to the family business—the one he'd never wanted to be part of—was getting louder and louder. Being a fourteen-hour flight away was no longer feasible. Then again, finding a position locally in his specialist field hadn't been feasible, either.

Timing was everything. If he'd applied for a paediatric post six months previously, with his background and experience he could almost have guaranteed his success. But all the desirable posts had been filled and it would be another six months before slots were available again.

This was a compromise. Only the compromise wasn't meant to kill him.

He saw a small boat in the distance. It seemed to be moving very slowly, creeping around the huge hull of the cruise ship as if it was crawling towards them like a tortoise. Every muscle in his body was starting to burn. His arms were like blocks of lead. The figures on the jetty were still shouting towards them and the shadow appeared again.

Gabriel struggled to turn his head as the brick wall loomed above them. All at once the danger became apparent. The sweeping current was taking them straight towards it and with Gabriel's hands caught tightly around the teenager's chest there was no opportunity to lift his hands and protect his head.

So much for being here to support his family.

And then everything went black.

Francesca was bored. Bored witless. Her mother's favourite British expression.

She smiled and nodded as someone walked past, shifting uncomfortably in the dress uniform. This was the one part of her job she hated. All the staff hated it. So much so, they drew straws each time the captain insisted one of the medical staff stand near the check-in desks in the terminal.

Standing in front of a pull-up banner of the *Silver Whisper* was not her idea of fun. The captain thought it made the medical staff look 'accessible'. She was going to have to talk to him about that.

She watched the passengers wandering in and looking in awe at the side view of the ship. As soon as they appeared the crew entertainment staff were all over them, thrusting brochures of trips the cruise ran at every port they stopped at. Francesca sighed and looked at her watch. This was going to be long day.

She glanced over her shoulder. None of the other senior staff were around. Who would notice if she slipped out for a few minutes? A smile danced across her lips. She crossed the terminal building in long strides, slipping out through a side door that took her down to the dock where the ship was moored.

The dock was jammed with suitcases and sweating crewmen struggling to load them on board. Her brain automatically switched into work mode—ticking off in her head who hadn't attended for their required medicals. She was going to have to crack the whip with the crew. Huge delivery crates of food were being wheeled up one of the gangways. It was amazing the amount of fresh food that was loaded at every port.

She wandered along the walkway, nodding greetings at several of the familiar crewmen, relishing the feel of the sun on her skin. Today, as every day, she'd applied sunscreen. But her Mediterranean skin rarely burned and the slightest touch of sun just seemed to enhance her glow.

This was the life. Working on a cruise ship had sounded like a dream at the time and a good sideways move. A chance to use all the skills she'd learned working in Coronary Care and A and E, along with the ability to use her advanced nurse practitioner status, and all in a relatively calm and safe environment.

But the long hours and constant nights on call were starting to wear her down. Thankfully she had a good supportive team to work with. A team that was slowly but surely helping her rebuild her confidence. The ship was a safe place to try and learn to trust her nursing instincts again. She'd once thought those instincts were good, but personal experience had taught her differently. It was time to start over and the ship seemed a good—if a little boring—place to start.

At the end of the day this was only supposed to be a temporary arrangement while she waited for her work visa for Australia to come through. But there had been delay after delay, with two months turning into three and then four. It seemed as if she'd been waiting for ever for the chance to spread her wings and go further afield. A chance to escape the memories of home.

'Nurse! Nurse!'

She turned swiftly towards the shout. It was at the end of the dock where a small crowd was gathered, pointing and looking out towards the sea. Francesca started running towards the shouts—one of the crew had obviously recognised her.

She could feel the adrenaline start to course through her veins. When had been the last time she'd dealt with an emergency? Would she be able to deal with one again? She'd started her staffing in a coronary care unit where cardiac arrests had been a daily occurrence. Then she'd moved to A and E to increase her skills. Expect the unexpected. That's what the sister she'd worked with had told her.

And she'd been right. From toddlers with a variety of household objects stuffed up their noses to RTA victims, she'd never known what would come through the door. Up until now she'd enjoyed the relative calm of the cruise ship. It could be a little mundane at times, dispensing seasickness tablets, dealing with upset stomachs and advising on sunburn. Maybe things were about to liven up?

She reached the edge of the dock and followed the pointing fingers to the two figures in the water. One looked like a child. She felt her stomach sink. The last thing she wanted was an injured child. A motorboat was approaching them and not before time. She winced as she watched the strong waves barrel them both into the port wall. Even though it was hundreds of yards away she could almost hear the crack.

The boat was almost on top of them and she watched as they dragged the child on board then struggled to reach the man, who had slipped beneath the waves. One crewman jumped into the water to help. Her heart thudded in her chest. Were they going to find him? The child was older than she'd first thought—probably a teenager—but the man?

Yes! They'd found him.

Oh, no. He was dressed from top to toe in white—an officer's uniform—and they were dragging his lifeless body out of the waves.

She started pushing the others aside. 'Let me through.' The boat was heading towards them. She turned to one of the crewmen, 'Go on board to the medical centre. Tell Dr Marsh I need some help. Tell them to bring a trolley and some resus equipment.' The crewman nodded and ran off.

Francesca noticed a woman sobbing near her and elbowed her way through the crowd. 'Are you okay?' she asked.

'My son Ryan. He was running along the walkway and he slipped. I got such a fright.' She gestured around about her. 'I couldn't find anything to throw to him. I couldn't find any lifebelts. And he can barely swim. Only a few lengths in a pool.' She shook her head furiously. 'Never in the sea.'

Francesca nodded, trying to take in all she'd heard. 'Who's the man?' she asked gingerly, dreading the answer she was about to hear.

The woman shook her head again. 'I've no idea. He appeared out of nowhere and dived straight in. Ryan was swept away so quickly, then he disappeared under the waves.' She was starting to sound frantic again. 'That man had to dive a few times before he finally found him.' The woman turned to face Francesca, her voice trembling. 'But what if he hadn't? What if he hadn't found my son…?' Her voice drifted off and her legs were starting to shake.

Francesca put a firm arm around her shoulders. 'Just hold on for a few minutes longer. Your son will probably be in shock when the boat reaches us. The sun may be shining but the water out there is pretty cold. How old is he?'

'He's thirteen.'

Francesca's brain was rapidly calculating the drugs she might need for an adolescent. It was always tricky to calculate for kids—everything was generally based on their weight as children came in all different shapes and sizes. And from her experience, at a time of emergency the last thing a parent remembered was their child's weight. It didn't matter. It was worth a try.

'Do you know how much Ryan weighs?'

The woman shook her head. Just as she'd suspected. If necessary, she'd have to make an educated guess when she saw him. Hopefully by then the rest of the team would have arrived.

Please don't let her have to resuscitate a child. She'd done it a few times in A and E and had been haunted by every occasion.

The motorboat was getting closer. Francesca recognised a few crewmen who must have commandeered some poor unsuspecting local's boat. Fear crept through her. The teenager was sitting at one side, a blanket flung around his shoulders, his face pale and water dripping from his hair. But the officer lay unmoving in the bottom of the boat—never a good sign. One of the other crewmen was leaning over him, so she couldn't see clearly what was going on.

The boat bobbed alongside them and she leapt over the gap to the other craft. She took a few seconds to check Ryan over. He was conscious, he was breathing and his pulse was strong. How he looked was another matter entirely. 'Get him onshore and get one of the medical team to assess him,' she instructed, before pushing the others out of her way to get to the man.

She glanced at his face and noted the three gold stripes on his shoulders. Not only an officer—but a senior officer. The uniform was familiar but the face wasn't. Maybe he wasn't one of theirs?

She was on autopilot now, the adrenaline bringing back all the things she'd thought she'd forgotten. She knelt by him, putting her head down next to his, her eyes level with his chest looking for the rise and fall that was distinctly lacking. Her fingers went to the side of his neck, checking for a carotid pulse. Nothing. She tipped his head back and had a quick check of his airway. Clear.

She didn't hesitate. She could do this in her sleep. On some occasions she almost *had* done this in her sleep. Some skills were never forgotten.

She took two deep breaths, forming a tight seal around his mouth with her own, and breathed into him, watching for the rise of his chest. She pulled at the white jacket, ripping down the front, and gold buttons pinged off and scattered around the bottom of the boat, revealing a plain white T-shirt underneath. She wasn't going to waste time trying to remove it. The firm muscles of his chest were clearly outlined and she had all the definition she needed.

She positioned her hands on his chest and started cardiac massage, counting in her head as she went. She was frantically trying to remember everything she could about drowning victims—an area she had little experience in. It seemed almost absurd when she was working on a cruise ship—but most passengers never came into contact with the sea. Didn't they have quite a good chance of survival if they were found quickly enough? She knew that there had been newspaper stories about children with hypothermia being pulled from frozen lakes and resuscitated successfully. But although this man's skin was cold, he wasn't hypothermic. There wasn't going to be any amazing news story here.

She kept going, conscious of voices behind her and shouted instructions. There was a thud as the boat rocked and a pair of black shiny shoes landed next to her. Her heart gave a sigh of relief. David Marsh was here to help her but she didn't stop what she was doing, leaning over and giving two long breaths again.

'Throw me over a defib and a bag and mask,' came the shout next to her.

Francesca kept going, the muscles in her arms straining as she started cardiac massage again. David was more than capable of organising everything around them.

She was counting again in her head. Twenty-two, twenty-three, twenty-four… *Come on*. She willed him to show some sign of recovery.

The handsome Italian features weren't lost on her. The dark brown hair, long eyelashes, strong chin, wide-framed body and muscled limbs. This man could be very impressive—if he was standing up.

David was pulling up the T-shirt that had been underneath his officer's jacket. 'I don't recognise him.' He squinted. 'Who on earth is he?'

She shook her head, 'I have no idea. Somehow I think I would have remembered this one.'

He slapped the pads on the muscular brown chest that Francesca was desperately trying not to notice and turned to switch on the machine. Then, before her eyes, the lean stomach muscles twitched. 'Wait!' she shouted.

She held her breath for a few seconds and then

he did it again. Twitched. And then coughed and spluttered everywhere. The Venetian water erupted from his lungs all over the deck around them and she hurried to help him on his side.

The monitor kicked into life, picking up his heart rate. His breathing was laboured and shallow. David read her thoughts and handed her over a cylinder of oxygen with a mask as he slipped a pulse oximeter on the man's finger.

Francesca bent over the man, blocking out the bright sunlight and shading his face from the nosy bystanders. She spoke in a low, calm voice. 'I'm holding an oxygen mask next to your face to help your breathing,' she said, praying he would understand because right now she had no idea if he spoke English. He opened his eyes. They were brown. Deep dark brown.

Wow.

But she must think purely as a professional. She must ignore everything about the Italian hunk they'd just pulled from the water. All the little things that would normally have sent shivers skittering down her spine.

She pulled her penlight from her pocket. This man probably had a head injury. She'd seen him being bounced off the port wall. She lifted his groggy eyelids and shone the light first in one eye and then the other. He gave the smallest flinch.

Pupils equal and reactive. She turned to David. 'We need to start proper neuro obs on this guy.'

He nodded. 'What happened?'

'He went in to rescue the boy. Once he'd got him the current carried them to the port wall and he was knocked unconscious. I think he was under the water for just over a minute.' Her hand reached around to the back of his head. His dark brown hair was wet but she could feel some abrasions at the back of his head. She pulled her hand back—blood.

'Can you give me something to patch this before we move him, please, David?'

David nodded and handed her some latex gloves and a dressing pad. 'Stretcher will be here in a minute. We'll get him onto the trolley and see if we can find some ID.'

Francesca hadn't lifted her head. He was still groggy. In all the TV shows she'd ever watched, victims of a near-drowning seemed to get up almost as soon as they were revived and walk off down the beach into the sunset. Usually hand in hand with their rescuer.

The thought of walking off into the sunset with this guy was definitely appealing. Like something out a fairy-tale. If only he would come round.

As a child she'd always loved the childhood fairy-tales Cinderella, Rapunzel, Snow White and Little Red Riding Hood. Her father had read them to her over and over again. Those were some of her fondest memories of him.

She leaned in a little closer to the man. If she really wanted to do a set of neurological observations on this guy then she needed to try and elicit some kind of response from him, a response to a painful stimulus.

'Wake up, Sleeping Beauty,' she whispered.

CHAPTER TWO

GABRIEL was in a dark place. Nothing. Nothingness. Then a sharp pain in his chest and the need to be sick. He coughed and spluttered, conscious that he was being pushed on his side but totally unable to assist. His head was thudding. His lungs felt as if they were burning. He heard a little hissing noise and felt a gentle, cool breeze on his face. What was that?

Someone tugged his eye open and shone a bright light at him. How dared they? Couldn't they see he just wanted to sleep? To be left alone for a few moments in this fuzzy place?

He felt a little pinch on his hand. Then another, more insistent.

'Ouch!' He was annoyed, irritated. Then he heard a soft, lilting voice with the strangest accent he'd heard in a while. 'Wake up, Sleeping Beauty. Are you with us?' Warm, soft breath tickled his cheek.

His eyelids flickered open. The sun was too bright.

Someone was trying to block the sunlight out.

Rats. It must be a dream. She was far too pretty for real life.

She was every guy's dream. A real-life modern-day princess. Mediterranean skin and dark eyes with tumbling brown curls. But something in this fairy-tale still wasn't working.

She spoke again. 'There we go, that's better.'

It was that accent. It didn't fit with his Mediterranean dream princess.

It confused him. Made his brain hurt. No—that wasn't his brain, that was his head.

He blinked again. The smell of the Adriatic Sea assaulting his senses. His skin was prickling. All of a sudden he felt uncomfortable. Something wasn't right. He was wet. Not just damp but soaked all over.

In the space of a few seconds the jigsaw puzzle pieces all fell into place. The young boy drowning, his attempt at saving him and the almighty crack to his head. He pushed himself up.

'Whoa, sailor. Take it easy there. You've had a bump on the head.'

'You can say that again,' he mumbled, squinting in the sunlight. 'And it's Doctor, not sailor.'

The princess's face broke into a wide perfect-toothed smile. 'Actually, I'll correct you there. On board, you're a sailor first, doctor second.'

David Marsh leaned forward, clutching some wet credentials in his hand. He held out his other hand. 'Well, this is an interesting way to meet our new boss. Gabriel Russo, I'm Dr David Marsh, your partner in crime. And this…' he nodded towards Francesca '…is Francesca Cruz, one of our nurse practitioners. But as you've just been mouth to mouth with each other, introductions seem a little late.' He signalled to the nearby crewmen. 'We're just going to get you on this stretcher and take you to the medical centre to check you over.'

Francesca felt a chill go down her spine at the name. She recognised it but couldn't for the life of her think why. She stared at him again. Was he vaguely familiar? She was sure she'd never met him, and with features like those he wasn't the kind of man you'd forget.

Gabriel looked horrified and shook his head, water flying everywhere. 'No stretcher. I'm fine.

I can walk.' He pushed his hands on the bottom of the boat and stood up, standing still for a few seconds to make sure his balance was steady.

His eyes found the thick rope securing the small boat to the quay before he stepped over the gap and back to the safety of solid ground. He spun round to face Francesca. 'How's the boy? Is he all right?' But he'd turned too quickly and he swayed.

She caught hold of his arm and gave him a cautious smile. 'He's on his way to the medical centre to be checked out. He was conscious, breathing but distinctly pale when he arrived. Now, how about I get you a wheelchair?'

'I don't do wheelchairs.'

She signalled over his shoulder. 'I can be very bossy when I want to be.'

Dr Marsh cut in, 'I can testify to that. Particularly if you think you're going to get the last chocolate. I should warn you in advance that's criminal activity in the medical centre.'

Gabriel felt pressure at the back of his legs as he thudded down into a wheelchair that had appeared out of thin air. 'I said I don't do chairs,' he growled.

'Let's argue about that later,' said Francesca as she swept the wheelchair along the dock.

The hairs on his arms were standing on end and he started to shiver—an involuntary action—a sign of shock. A few seconds later a space blanket was placed around his shoulders.

He grudgingly pulled it around him, noting the efficiency of his new staff and the easy rapport and teamwork—all good signs. Within a few seconds his nurse appeared to have walked the hundreds of yards along the dock and was pushing him up the gangway.

This was a nightmare. The worst way possible to meet your new staff. Yet another reason he should never have taken this job.

She seemed to turn automatically to her left, heading toward the service elevators. Gabriel felt mild panic start to build in his chest. Could this day get any worse?

Then she quickly veered off to the right. 'Where are we going?' he growled.

'To the medical centre. We're already on Deck Four so it will only take a couple of minutes.' If she was annoyed by his tone there was no sign.

Gabriel heaved a sigh of relief and settled back

in the chair. He'd be fine once he got something for this headache and was out of these wet clothes. Then he could get started.

The chair turned sharply into the modern medical centre. Consulting rooms, treatment rooms, in-patient beds and state-of-the-art diagnostics and emergency equipment. He knew the spec for this place off by heart—it was impressive, even by his exacting standards.

She wheeled him through to one of the rooms and pulled the curtains around the bed, pushing the brake on the wheelchair. She disappeared for a second and came back with a towel and set of scrubs.

Francesca's brain was whirring. Gabriel Russo. Why was that name so familiar? Then it hit her like a ton of bricks falling from the sky. She *had* seen him before. Only last time he'd been wearing a pair of white designer swimming trunks and been perched on the edge of a multi-million-pound yacht, his arm lazily flung around the shoulders of her bikini-clad friend Jill.

The Italian stallion, Jill had called him and that picture had adorned her flatmate's bedside cabinet until one night when a sobbing Jill had phoned Francesca at 3:00 a.m. to come and pick her up.

Francesca would never forget the sight of Jill in her sodden green designer gown, her hair plastered around her face and tears running like rivulets down her cheeks after Gabriel had flung her out of his penthouse flat.

Jill had been broken-hearted over his treatment of her and had taken a good few weeks to get over him—a long time for Jill.

And Francesca had waited a long time, too—to tell this man exactly what she thought of him. He was alive. He was breathing. His heart rate was sound. After a few general observations for head injuries he should be fine. There was a determined edge to her chin; it would be criminal to waste this opportunity. And she had absolutely no intention of doing so.

Something was wrong. Something had changed. He could sense it immediately; the tension in the air was palpable. Right now, all he wanted to do was climb into that pristine white bed, close his eyes and lose this thumping headache.

But the soft side of his Mediterranean princess had vanished and she was staring at him as if he were something she'd just trodden on.

Or maybe he was imagining it? Maybe the resuscitation and head knock had affected him more than he'd thought?

'You're Gabriel Russo.'

Gabriel's pounding head jerked in response to the sharp tone in her voice. He wasn't imagining it. 'I thought we had established that.'

'No, you're Gabriel Russo, *Italian stallion*.' She lifted her fingers in the air, making the quotation mark signs, wrinkled her nose and then continued, 'Stinking love rat. You used to date my friend Jill—until you threw her out of your apartment in London at 3:00 a.m. in the pouring rain.'

'No one's ever called me Italian stallion to my face before.' He felt almost amused. The nickname had been plastered across the press often enough. He wasn't used to being blindsided. Then again, he wasn't used to being resuscitated.

Jill. The name flickered through his brain. He'd certainly dated more than his fair share of beautiful women and he'd worked all over the world. Something fell into place. London. No. Let's hope she wasn't talking about *that* Jill. Just what he needed—a misguided, loyal friend. If his head wasn't thumping so much this could almost be funny. Not only that—Ms Misguided was a knockout. A beautiful work colleague would never be a problem. But an angry, venomous one would be. This was a small team. They had to work together. It could be badly affected by two people who didn't get on.

She wasn't finished. 'But I bet plenty of women have called you a heartbreaker before.'

'Have we met?' His eyes ran up and down her body and she felt a prickle of disgust—he'd almost mirrored her thoughts from earlier. 'I think I'd remember.'

A few minutes before she'd had nice thoughts drifting about her head about their new doctor. She'd thought he was handsome. She'd thought he was fit. She'd even thought… No. She hadn't. She couldn't possibly have.

He frowned. 'Jill? Who was she again? Remind me.'

Francesca felt rage build inside her. Arrogant so-and-so. The palm of her hand itched—she wanted it to come into contact with his perfect cheek.

'Six years ago. London. Blonde model. You took her on your yacht for the weekend.'

'Oh, *that* Jill.' His frown deepened, puckering little lines around his eyes. He turned away, pulling his muddied jacket and T-shirt over his head, and she sensed it was on purpose. She tossed the scrubs and towel onto the bed beside him.

'Yes, *that* Jill.' The volume of her voice increased in proportion to her rage. 'The one you dumped in the middle of the night in the pouring rain outside your flat. What kind of a man does that?'

He whipped around, the muddied jacket and T-shirt clenched in his fists, leaving his wide brown chest right in front of her eyes. The fury in her voice couldn't match the venom in his eyes. 'What kind of a man does that?' he growled.

She gulped. He was half-dressed, his shoulder muscles tense, his bare abdomen rigid. If they were shooting an action movie right now he would be the perfect poster-boy hero.

All of a sudden the room felt much smaller.

Maybe it was the six-foot-four presence. All trembling muscle and eyes shooting fireballs in her direction.

She could feel every hair on her body stand on end. And she hated it.

Because amongst the repulsion there was something else she was feeling—something more—and it went against every principle she had.

She pushed all those thoughts aside. If she ignored them then they weren't actually *there*.

He still hadn't answered. Probably because he was incoherent with rage.

'What are you doing here anyway? Aren't you supposed to be some billionaire-type doctor? You don't actually have to work for a living, do you? Why on earth would you be working on a cruise ship?'

He shook his head, almost imperceptibly. What a surprise. All the usual assumptions, misunderstandings and wrong conclusions. All the things he went to pains to shake off. Normally he wouldn't care what some stranger thought of him. But this stranger was part of his team *and* she was going to have to learn who was boss around here—hardly an ideal start. 'Some things you wouldn't understand.' He leaned against the side of the bed, and could feel the pressure inside his head increase.

'Try me.'

Something flashed across his face. He took a deep breath. 'How well do you know Jill?'

'She is my friend. She was my flatmate in London. We lived together for six months.'

'Six years ago?' There was an edge to his voice—almost as if he couldn't believe someone had been friends with Jill that long.

'Yes. We don't live together any more but we keep in touch.' She scanned her brain, trying to think of the last time she'd heard from Jill—maybe a week or more?

'And how many times did you have to pick her up heartbroken in the middle of the night?'

'Once.' Not strictly true. But he was beginning to look too smug. There was a lot not to like. He was too handsome and too sure of himself. And she didn't like that look on his face—as if he knew something she didn't.

'Jill is a really good friend of mine. She helped

me when I needed it most. Make no mistake about where my loyalty lies, Gabriel.'

Those words didn't even touch what Jill had done for her. When her father had died, Jill had dropped everything and flown straight up from London to Glasgow. She'd organised the funeral, dealt with the post-mortem, sorted out the insurance and the contents of the house—all things that Francesca couldn't possibly have dealt with. Jill had been her rock.

In the past their relationship had always felt uneven, as if Francesca was constantly running after Jill and taking care of her. But when the chips had been down Jill had more than risen to the challenge. Francesca couldn't have got through it without her.

'How long are you here for?'

'I haven't even done my first shift and you're trying to get rid of me?'

She shrugged.

'As long as I want. I took this job at short notice—someone had broken their contract—so I was pretty much offered what I wanted. It's up to me to decide how long I want to stay.'

Great. Who knew how long she would be stuck

with him? 'You didn't answer the original question. Why would a billionaire doc like you want to be working on a cruise ship?'

He waved his hand dismissively. 'Family stuff.'

It was the first interesting thing he'd said.

Yip. The walls in the room were definitely closing in on her. This was her worst nightmare. Working with this man every day was going to play havoc with her senses and her principles. She hated the fact that under other circumstances she might like him. She hated the fact she'd almost flirted with him.

'I know you'll have some clean uniforms in your quarters but how about putting these on right now?' She pointed to the scrubs. She wrinkled her nose at the ruined jacket and T-shirt, still in his hand. 'I don't care how good the laundry staff are here, they're not going to be able to save *those*.'

Gabriel stood up, his legs feeling firmer than before. He hadn't even considered his appearance. The pristine white uniform he was holding was covered in remnants of brown sludge. His body hadn't fared much better. From the port wall perhaps? She was right, no matter what the

TV adverts pretended to show, no washing powder on the planet could sort this out.

He grabbed the towel to rub his hair, momentarily forgetting the reason he was there and wincing as the edge of the towel caught his wound.

'Easy, tiger.' Francesca pushed him down onto the edge of the bed. 'Let me do that.' She took the towel from his hands and gently dried around the edges.

'Stop fussing,' he muttered, trying to swat her hand away. 'I need a shower.'

Francesca was doing her best to push her anger aside. She had a job to do. Whether she liked him or not, he was a patient—one she'd just resuscitated and with a head injury. She was a good nurse. This was straightforward. She could do this. 'Right now I'm in charge—not you. You can go in the shower when I say so.' She stuck a tympanic thermometer in his ear. 'I'm going to do a full set of neurological observations on you, then clean that head wound and either glue or stitch it.' She glanced at the reading on the thermometer. 'You're still cold. We're going to heat you up a bit first.' She pulled a blanket from one of the nearby cupboards.

Gabriel sighed. At least she was an efficient nurse, even if she was smart-mouthed and hated his guts. 'Where's Dr Marsh?'

She peered around the edge of the door. 'He and Katherine are dealing with the teenager. Children get priority. I'm sure you'd agree with that.'

The child, of course. What was he thinking? There was a child to be attended to. 'I should go and check him over.' He tried to push his blanket off, but she laid her hand firmly on his shoulder.

The constricting feeling across his chest was almost instant. Paediatrics—children were his whole reason for being a doctor. There was no way he'd watch a child suffer. He couldn't stand the thought that there was a child in the next room requiring attention while he was being pushed onto a bed.

It made him feel useless. It pushed him into dark places imprinted on his mind. Memories of long ago. Of a child with a scream that sent shivers down his spine. Feelings he'd spent his whole professional career trying to avert.

He pushed himself off the bed again.

'Gabriel.'

Her face was right in front of his, her large brown eyes looking him straight on and her voice firm.

'Ryan is fine. David Marsh is more than capable of looking after a shocked teenager. Maybe—just maybe—if we were resuscitating him, like we did with you, I might let you go and assist. But this isn't an emergency situation. You're not needed. You're not even officially on duty. Right now you're a patient, not a doctor. And a cranky one at that. You'd better hope that your head injury is making you cranky because if that's your normal temperament you won't last five minutes in here.

She was right. The rational part of his brain that was still functioning *knew* she was right. But his heart was ruling his head. He was cursing himself for not paying more attention to the port wall. He shouldn't have dived straight in, he should have taken a few more seconds to get his bearings. Then maybe he could have protected Ryan and stopped him from slipping from his arms.

They could hear rapid chatter next door. She obviously didn't realise his background in paediatrics. It was hardly surprising. Six years ago he'd been just about to pick his speciality and he'd dumped Jill before he'd made his final choice.

'You should stay where you are. I'm going to attach you to a monitor for a few hours. You, sir, are going to do exactly as I say—whether you like it or not.' She pulled the wires from the nearby monitor. 'I'm not the pushover Jill was,' she murmured.

Gabriel felt a weight settle on his chest again. For a second he'd seen a little glimpse of humour from her. For a second he'd thought maybe she didn't hate him quite as much as it seemed. This was the last thing he needed—some smart-mouthed nurse with a load of preconceived ideas him. How close was she to Jill? Hopefully she didn't have any of the same tendencies—that could be disastrous.

Every part of his body was beginning to ache and if he didn't get something for this headache soon he was going to erupt.

It was almost as if she'd read his mind. 'I'll

give you something for your headache in a few
moments. I want to have a clear baseline set
of neuro obs and I can't give you anything too
strong—I don't want to dull your senses.' There
was a hint of humour in her voice, the implication that his senses were already dulled crystal
clear.

It was just about as much as he could take.

'Enough about me. What about you?' he
snapped. 'What's with the accent? Where are
you from?'

The unexpected question caught her unawares
and she jolted. She put the unattached wires
down and her brow wrinkled. She bent to shine
her penlight in his eyes again, satisfying herself
that his pupils were equal and reactive.

'I'm from Scotland.' She straightened up.

'You don't look like you're from Scotland,'
he mumbled as he dropped the towel he'd been
using to dry himself, revealing the taut abdominal muscles, and pulled the scrub top over his
head. 'You look like a native. And what were
you doing in London?'

'I could be offended by that,' she said quickly,
placing one hand on her hip as she tried to drag

her eyes away from his stomach. Was this his natural response? Was he normally so blunt? Or was this an altered response that she should be concerned about? She had no background knowledge on which to base a judgment. Should she just take for granted that he could be quite rude?

He'd paused, half-dressed, and was watching her. Watching the way her eyes were looking at his taut abdomen. She felt the colour flooding into her cheeks. There was no point averting her eyes, she'd been well and truly caught. She could be cheeky, too.

'Put those away. You'll give a girl a complex. And they'll need to go, too.' She pointed at his muddied underwear and handed him the scrub bottoms, averting her eyes for a few seconds to allow him some privacy. She slid her hand up inside his scrub top to attach the leads to his chest. His brown, muscled chest.

Time to change the subject. 'My parents were from Trapetto, a fishing village in Sicily. But I was brought up in Scotland. I'm a Glasgow girl through and through.' She waved her hand. 'And don't even try to speak to me in Italian. I'm not fluent at all—I know enough for emergencies and how to order dinner but that's it.'

'Didn't you speak Italian at home?'

His voice brought her back to reality. 'Rarely. There wasn't much call for it in Glasgow.'

Her eyelids had lowered, as if this wasn't a conversation she wanted to get into. Why was that?

Francesca picked up his dirty clothes. 'I take it you're okay if I dump these?'

He nodded and shifted on the bed, frowning at his attached leads. 'So what are you doing here, Francesca?'

She froze, a little shocked by the bluntness of the question. This guy was going to take a bit of getting used to.

She frowned at him, knowing her brow was wrinkled and it wasn't the most flattering of looks. 'What on earth are you talking about?'

There it was again, that little hint of something—but not quite obvious.

'I would have thought that was obvious. I'm here working as an ANP. Maybe I should check that head knock of yours again.'

His eyebrows lifted. 'I'm curious what a young,

well-qualified nurse like you is doing here.' His hand swept outwards to the surrounding area.

She felt a little shiver steal down her spine. Nosy parker.

She kept her voice steady. 'You mean here…' she spread her arms out and spun round '…in this state-of-the-art medical complex, in the middle of the Mediterranean, with a different port every day and a chance to see the world?'

She planted her hands on her hips and looked at him as defiantly as she could. She was stating the obvious. The thing that any website would quote for prospective job-seekers. It was a cop-out and she knew it. But she didn't like the way he'd asked the question. It was as if he'd already peered deep inside her and knew things she didn't want anyone else to know.

'I'm just curious. Your family is in Glasgow. And yet, you're here…' His voice tailed off. Almost as if he was contemplating the thought himself.

Something inside her snapped. Were all Italians as old-fashioned as him?

'My family isn't in Glasgow any more. Get a life, Gabriel. Isn't a girl allowed to spread her wings and get a job elsewhere? Maybe I'm trying to connect with my roots in Sicily. Maybe I was just bored in Glasgow. Maybe I want to see the world. Or it could just be that I'm killing time until I get my visa to Australia. I thought cruise ships would be fun. Truth be told, so far I've found it all a bit boring.' The words were out before she'd thought about it. Out before she had a chance to take them back.

She cringed. He was her boss. He was her *brand-new* boss, who had no idea about her skills, experience and competency level—probably the only things that could be her saving grace right now. How to win friends and influence people. Not.

She pushed the dirty clothes inside a plastic disposal bag, 'I'll get rid of these,' she muttered as she turned to leave.

This was going to be nightmare. This ship was huge. Big enough for two thousand, six hundred passengers and five hundred staff. But this medical centre? Not so big. And the staff worked very closely together. Some days the medical centre felt positively crowded.

And the last thing she needed was to be stuck

with some playboy doc. A pain shot through her chest. The last time she'd been distracted by a playboy doc it had had a devastating effect on her family life, causing irreparable damage. She could *not* allow that to happen again, no matter what the circumstances.

Every part of her body was buzzing. She hadn't even had a chance to think about what had happened today. She'd resuscitated someone.

Someone who could, potentially, have died if she hadn't taken those actions.

The thought of dealing with a death again horrified her. It didn't matter that she was a nurse. Her circumstances had changed. Everything had changed.

Deaths weren't supposed to happen on cruise ships. Working here was part of her safety net— keeping her away from the aspects of her job she couldn't deal with any more.

And now him.

On top of everything else.

She leaned back against the wall. There was no two ways about it.

This ship wasn't big enough for the two of them.

CHAPTER THREE

FRANCESCA'S fingers thumped furiously on the keyboard.

Hey babe!
You'll never believe who I'm working with right now—Gabriel Russo. Yes, the very one. And he's every bit the conceited billionaire boy that he was six years ago. It took me a few minutes to work out who he was—probably because I had to re-suscitate him first—but needless to say, once I'd reminded him I was your flatmate you could cut the atmosphere in here with a knife.

Cruise ships might look huge in real life but the reality is, when you can't stand to be around someone, they seem very small.

Haven't seen you in a while, so hope you're doing well.

In the meantime living in hope he'll fall over-board,

Fran xx

'Busy?'

The voice, cutting through the dark medical centre in the dead of night, made her jump. Couldn't she get any peace from this man?

She could barely tolerate being in the same room as him. What's more, he constantly appeared at her shoulder, checking over what she'd done. And for someone whose confidence was already at rock bottom it was more than a little irritating.

There were always two crew members on call at night—one for the passengers and one for the crew. One week had passed and this was Gabriel's first official night on call and Francesca had drawn the short straw of babysitting him.

She spun around in her chair to face him. He had his black medical bag in his hand. 'I'm waiting for one of the crew members to meet me,' she said. 'She's complaining of abdominal pain.'

'Need a hand?'

Francesca bit her tongue to stop her saying the words that were dancing around her head right now. *Over my dead body* probably wouldn't go down that well with her boss.

'No, I'm fine, thanks.' She pasted a smile on

her face and gestured towards his bag. 'You look busy enough anyway. Lots of passenger call-outs?'

He nodded, rubbing his hand across his eyes. 'Three in the last hour. All for really ridiculous things. Please tell me this isn't a normal night.'

Francesca smiled. If it had been anyone else she would have told him about the 'cougar list' currently taped inside one of the cupboard doors in the treatment room.

The list of well-known passengers—mainly women in their forties and fifties—who developed symptoms requiring a cabin call whenever a new, young doctor came on board. She could bet in the last hour Gabriel had seen a lot of skin and satin negligees.

Not all the passengers changed every week or every fortnight. A certain select group seemed to spend a large part of their life cruising. It was not unusual to have the same passengers on board for four to six weeks at a time. Sometimes they swapped to another ship for a month and then came back to the *Silver Whisper* again.

The 'cougar list' had been started by Kevin, one of the nurses, after he'd noticed a sharp rise in callouts whenever a new doctor started. It was really just a warning list to give the person on call the opportunity to decide if they wanted to take the other crew member on duty with them. She would tell him about the list—really, she would—just not yet.

Francesca was sure that Gabriel could handle a few coy looks. After all, hadn't he spent his life chasing women, collecting them like trophies and then unceremoniously dumping them? This should be a breeze for him.

'Here, have a look at this.' She handed him the communiqué she'd been given requesting details about the rescue at Venezia Passegeri. Apparently the media were keen to run a story. 'They're a little late but maybe they were short of news.'

A dark shadow passed over his face as his eyes flew over the page. 'Absolutely not. No names. I don't want to talk about last week. Make sure the communications officer understands.'

She shrugged, a little surprised by his reaction. 'The cruise line probably wants the publicity,' she suggested. 'What's the problem? You're used to being in the news.'

'No!' He looked furious. He crumpled the piece of paper in his hand and threw it deftly into the wastepaper bin. She smirked. *Message received, loud and clear.*

Was this man temperamental? Maybe his snappiness after his head injury hadn't been the result of the accident. His questions to her had been a little blunt. He certainly wasn't exhibiting all the traits Jill had told her about of the flirtatious, playboy doctor. Gabriel Russo seemed to be a wolf in doctor's clothing. And the thought intrigued her.

Katherine had complained bitterly last week that Gabriel wasn't the best of patients—apparently she'd had to practically pin him to the bed to monitor his neuro obs overnight after his head injury. He'd been furious when Dr Marsh had insisted he be monitored overnight and it had been a relief to them all when he'd been given a clean bill of health the following morning and allowed to take on normal duties.

His pager sounded again and he sighed, picking up his medical bag and heading for the door. 'If I'm not back in an hour page me.' He hesitated for a second, his brown eyes connecting with hers. 'Please.'

Francesca couldn't help but smile. Maybe he was finally catching onto the cougar brigade.

She turned back to the computer and pulled up the file for the crew member she was about to meet.

The notes were limited. Elena Portiss, twenty-seven, from Spain, working on board as a bartender, with a declared past medical history of endometriosis.

She'd phoned ten minutes earlier saying her abdominal pain was worse than usual—bad abdominal pain was not uncommon in a woman with a history of endometriosis.

There was a noise behind her and Francesca stood up and flicked the switch, lighting up the medical unit.

'Elena?'

The young woman nodded.

Francesca was immediately struck by how pale the girl was. Her pale blue eyes were dull and lifeless, her normally tanned skin pallid and slightly waxy.

'Come in here.' Francesca walked into the

nearby room and gestured Elena towards one of the examination trolleys. She worked quickly, checking her temperature, blood pressure and pulse. 'You have endometriosis?' Francesca spoke slowly, taking care in case there was any difficulty in language.

Elena nodded. Francesca noted that her hands were positioned carefully over her stomach, obviously trying to keep her pain in check. 'It was diagnosed last year after I had very painful periods.' She lifted her shirt and pointed to a little scar next to her belly button. 'I had a camera in there.'

Francesca nodded. If Elena had had a laparoscopy done and the diagnosis confirmed then it was likely that her symptoms were related to her endometriosis.

'Do you normally use painkillers?' Elena nodded and fumbled in her bag, pulling out a battered box with the name written in Spanish. Francesca took the box, looking at it and writing the name down in the notes. It was a commonly used non-steroidal anti-inflammatory drug that was effective in treating endometriosis.

'We will be able to give you something similar,' she reassured Elena, 'but the box may look a little different. Have you tried anything else?'

Elena pulled a second, slightly more battered cardboard box from her bag. 'I stopped taking these,' she said, 'as they made me feel unwell.' As she didn't recognise the name on the box Francesca opened it and pulled out the foil strip with the twenty-eight tablets enclosed. Around half were missing and she realised immediately what they were. Oral contraceptives were commonly used to treat endometriosis in women who weren't trying to start a family. They worked by regulating the hormone levels to stop the production of oestrogen in the body. Without exposure to oestrogen, the endometrial tissue could be reduced and this helped to ease symptoms.

'Do you remember when your last period was?' Francesca asked.

'I'm not sure. I had some bleeding yesterday and a little this morning, but it wasn't much.'

'I'm so sorry, but I'm going to have to get a urine specimen from you. Do you think you can manage to go to the toilet for me?'

Elena grimaced as Francesca helped her to the toilet. It only took a few minutes before she was back on the couch and Francesca reattached her to the blood-pressure cuff. BP was ninety over sixty. Hypotensive. Colour poor. Alarm bells started to go off inside Francesca's head.

The amount of pain that Elena was exhibiting was more than would be expected. Elena nodded, still clutching her stomach.

Francesca's spider sense was tingling. Her instinct—the thing she'd thought she'd lost.

This wasn't right. This didn't *feel* right. Elena's pain seemed too severe and too localised to be endometriosis. Francesca knew that endometriosis was a painful condition in which the endometrial cells that would normally be present within the lining of the womb could be deposited in other areas around the body. These cells were still influenced by the female hormones and could cause pain in various areas, particularly around the pelvis.

And she knew how painful it could be—one of her friends spent a few days every month doubled up in bed. But this just didn't add up.

She checked the urine sample for infection and it was clear. Francesca opened the nearby cupboard and pulled out another test. It was only a hunch and she could be wrong. Using a little pipette she dropped a few drops of urine onto the test and checked her watch. A little line appeared.

Her heart gave a flutter in her chest. She hadn't been wrong and for a second she felt almost elated. Then common sense pulled her back to reality.

She needed help. And no matter how much he irritated her, she knew who to call.

The pager sounded again.

Gabriel was annoyed. What would be the reason for this ridiculous callout? A stubbed toe? A grazed elbow? He was going to have serious words with the team in the morning if this was what they normally dealt with.

He glanced at the number on the pager. The medical centre. Francesca. Now, that *was* a surprise. She'd looked as if she'd rather set her hair on fire than ask him for help earlier.

And as for the media request…

It made his blood boil. His family were constantly in the paper—particularly in Italy. With the words 'tragic' usually appearing in the second sentence. Twenty-five years ago the media had been all over them and their 'tragic' loss. Every time they were mentioned in the press it was all raked over again.

The last thing they needed was more painful reminders.

Didn't they get that the loss of Dante was imprinted on them for life, seared on their very souls?

Gabriel had never once given an interview to a journalist.

Correction. Gabriel had never *knowingly* given an interview to a journalist. The ugly remnants of a faked past relationship by an aspiring reporter burned hard. That, and his experience with Jill and a few others like her, told him that women weren't to be trusted. Under any circumstances.

It only took him a few moments to reach the medical centre.

'What's wrong?'

Francesca was waiting at the door for him, some notes in her hands and a worried expression on her face.

She thrust the notes towards him. 'Elena Portiss, twenty-seven, severe abdominal pain, past history of endometriosis.'

'Have you given her some analgesics?'

'Not yet.'

'Why not?'

She hesitated just for a second. 'Because she's pregnant and she doesn't know it. I think it may be an ectopic pregnancy,' she said tentatively.

Gabriel's eyes skimmed over the notes in front of him. He'd no idea why she looked like a deer currently caught in the headlights. She'd done everything he would have expected. 'Let's find out.'

Francesca caught his arm as he walked past her. 'I haven't given her any indication about what I think may be wrong.' Gabriel caught the worried expression in her eyes. He understood completely. Endometriosis was frequently associated with infertility. To tell the patient that she was pregnant but that the pregnancy was ectopic would be a devastating blow. He strode through to the treatment room and spoke to Elena, who was lying on the examination couch, her face still racked in pain.

'Hello, Elena,' he said confidently, 'my name

is Dr Russo. I'm one of the ship's doctors. Nurse Cruz has asked that I take a little look at you.' He shook Elena's trembling hand. As he placed his hands very gently on her stomach he noticed her visibly flinching. 'I promise you, I will be very gentle.'

He moved lightly across her abdomen, pressing gently with his fingertips from one side to the other. 'Where is the pain worse? Here? Here?'

Elena shook her head tensely, and then grimaced again in pain as his fingers reached her right side. The clinical signs were all present. She was pale, hypotensive, with lower abdominal tenderness and distension. That, together with a positive pregnancy test, gave an almost conclusive picture.

Francesca watched him from the corner of the room. Had she been wrong to mention her tentative diagnosis? Other doctors might have thought she was stepping on their toes to make such a suggestion.

But Gabriel hadn't even blinked. He didn't seem offended or annoyed with her suggestion. His only concern seemed to be for the patient.

Given the hostility between them it could have

been a perfect opportunity for him to take her to task.

But apparently not. This man wasn't exactly how she'd imagined him to be.

'Okay, that's me finished.' He took his hands from Elena's abdomen and stood next to her.

'Do you know the date of your last period, Elena?'

She shook her head miserably. 'I have been bleeding on and off for several months. I can't say for sure. I was taking the Pill, too, but it made me feel unwell, so I stopped. Then I had some light bleeding yesterday. I'm not sure when my last period was.'

Gabriel nodded, 'That's okay'. He turned to Francesca. 'Can you check her BP and pulse again for me, please, and draw some bloods? I'll need her urea and electrolytes, but more importantly a full blood count, please.'

Francesca nodded and set the monitor to retake Elena's blood pressure while she opened the nearby drawer to find the blood bottles. Once the blood pressure had been recorded she removed the cuff and replaced it with a tourniquet to facilite taking some blood. It only took her a matter of seconds to locate a vein. 'Just a little prick,' she said to Elena as she gently slid the needle into the vein and attached the bottle to collect the blood samples. Francesca released the clip on the tourniquet, letting it spring apart, relieving the pressure on Elena's arm. She placed the needle in the nearby sharps box and gave Gabriel a quick glance as she left the room. 'I'll phone Kevin and get him to do the blood results for us.'

She wondered if he realised how quickly her heart was beating in her chest. Elena's blood count would be a good indicator of whether her diagnosis was correct or not.

It could also prove that her instincts were still completely off.

The medical centre was equipped with a wide range of laboratory equipment that allowed the staff to carry out many diagnostic tests that were essential to diagnosing and treating patients. Kevin arrived a few minutes later, hair mussed, took the blood samples and prepared them for testing. When she returned to the room Gabriel was sitting next to the examination trolley, talking to Elena. Francesca could see the serious expression on his face and watched as he gently took Elena's hand to explain her condition. Gabriel was surprising her. He was taking time to talk to Elena, to hold her hand and explain clearly what was happening. For some reason she found it almost the opposite of what she'd expected. This was a man who'd flung her friend out on the street at three o'clock in the morning yet here he was as a doctor, doing everything he should and showing empathy for his patient. In her head that just didn't fit. Her curiosity was piqued.

She listened quietly in the background.

'Elena,' he said gently, 'I think it is likely that you're having an ectopic pregnancy.' He noticed the complete confusion on her face, and realised she hadn't really understood. 'Your urine test shows that you are pregnant—but this is not a normal pregnancy.'

'But I can't be pregnant—I have endometriosis—it's not possible for me to be pregnant.' Her face was filled with shock.

'It is possible,' Gabriel continued carefully. 'Have you had sex in the last six weeks?'

Elena nodded numbly.

'Although your condition makes it difficult to

conceive, it is not impossible. It is likely that because you were taking the contraceptive pill you've become unclear about when your next period was due. Your urine test is definitely positive. However, the pain and discomfort that you are feeling makes it likely that, instead of implanting in the womb, the fertilised egg has implanted in your Fallopian tube.' He picked up a nearby book with pictures of the female reproductive system and pointed to the various areas, showing her where the fertilised ovum had likely reached.

The medical staff often used these clear diagrammatic books to explain conditions to crew members of different nationalities. 'The embryo can't develop within this confined space and causes bleeding and pain. Sometimes the tube can rupture and that can be very serious. But in all cases the pregnancy can't continue.'

He waited for a moment, until he could tell that Elena had processed the information he had given her. Elena started sobbing uncontrollably. Gabriel had been right. The news of a pregnancy, followed by the news that it was ectopic and couldn't produce a baby, had devastated her.

'What happens now?' she asked.

Gabriel stood up from the chair. 'We have to watch you very closely so we are going to admit you to our intensive care unit. I'll put up some fluids and give you some pain relief. One of our nurses will come and take some more bloods from you in the next few hours. I will have to arrange for you to go to hospital at the next port.'

Kevin appeared and handed Gabriel the blood results. Haemoglobin eight point seven. Gabriel glanced in Francesca's direction. No words were needed. They both knew that was much lower than normal for a woman of her age and more than likely an indicator of some internal bleeding.

Francesca felt the flush of relief rush through her system. She'd been right. For once her instincts had been good. If things weren't so serious for their patient right now she would run outside and breathe a big sigh of relief.

When had been the last time she'd felt like this? The last time she'd had real confidence in her abilities as a nurse?

After her initial meeting with Gabriel, she

couldn't have blamed him if he'd ignored her instincts at all. But he hadn't.

He hadn't even really questioned her. He'd taken her at her word and just moved on. He hadn't even *doubted* her. Why?

This virtual stranger had more faith in her than she had in herself. Maybe there was more to him than met the eye.

Sure enough, they'd been mouth to mouth before, but he couldn't remember any of that—could he?

Francesca administered the analgesia and then moved through to the intensive care unit to set up the bed and equipment that would be needed.

Gabriel came over and placed a hand on her shoulder, his forefinger touching the delicate skin at the side of her neck. She felt herself flinch but not in displeasure, just at the electricity of his warm touch. The tingles running down her spine were making her lose her concentration. He leaned towards her with a wide smile, showing his perfect teeth. 'That was an impressive call, Francesca,' he praised. 'Not one that everyone would have recognised—and that includes medical staff. Her initial symptoms could easily have been written off as her ongoing endo-metriosis.' He nodded his head in appreciation. 'What made you think twice?'

'Instinct,' came the immediate reply, followed by a loose shrug of the shoulders. 'It just didn't seem right.' *Instinct.* The word had come to her lips so easily. Almost automatically. Too bad she hadn't always trusted her instincts. Maybe then she would still be in Glasgow.

Maybe then she would still have some of her family left.

Something else stirred inside her. He was praising her. He was giving her the credit for the diagnosis. And it spread a warm feeling through her insides. Maybe she should be more confident about herself—the way she used to be.

'I've spoken to the captain. We are due to dock in Piraeus tomorrow at nine. He's told me that if there are problems he will probably be able to arrange a quicker dock time, as long as we give him some notice. He could alter the speed accordingly as the actual physical sea miles could be covered more quickly if it was necessary. Who will be looking after the patient?'

'I will.' There was no way she wanted anyone

else to look after Elena. She wanted to see this through.

The next port was in Athens, Greece, and although the actual distance between Venice and Athens was not huge, they often spent full days at sea. This gave passengers time to adjust to the feel of the ocean and a chance to find their way around the boat. They'd already circled the Med once and were repeating the journey again.

Kevin appeared at the door. 'She's complaining of shoulder-tip pain now, Dr Russo.' Gabriel crossed the room quickly. Shoulder-tip pain could be a serious sign. It could mean that there was internal bleeding into the abdominal cavity that was irritating the diaphragm. This was usually a sign that the ectopic pregnancy had ruptured and would require surgery—something they were not equipped to do at sea. He spent a few more moments examining Elena, while Francesca rechecked her pulse and blood pressure.

'Pulse one-ten, BP eighty-five over fifty.' Her hand reached automatically towards the intravenous fluids that were hanging next to the bed. 'Do you want these increased?' He nodded and she automatically adjusted the controls on the machine. It was clear from her symptoms that Elena's ectopic pregnancy had ruptured and she was bleeding internally. Her pulse had risen and blood pressure dropped, which meant she was going into hypovolaemic shock. Increasing her intravenous fluids would only be a minor stop-gap in trying to treat her. She really needed surgery.

Gabriel stood up swiftly. 'I'm going to notify the captain and arrange an emergency evac.'

Francesca watched his retreating back. She was impressed by how calm he was. She hadn't been able to ascertain whether Gabriel had much experience of being at sea, but on more than one occasion she had seen other doctors panic at the thought of dealing with a surgical emergency on board. Most doctors were used to working in large general hospitals that had all the services they needed at their fingertips. Working at sea was entirely different. Making a wrong decision could cost a patient their life, but Gabriel appeared to be taking it all in his stride.

There was the tiniest flutter in her stomach. If,

for any reason, they couldn't get Elena off the ship there was a possibility she could die.

Francesca pushed the thought from her mind. She couldn't even contemplate anything like that. She couldn't bear the thought of having to deal with the death of a patient. Not now.

She watched as he pressed the button on the phone to end his first call and start another. 'The captain will go with my decision. We can't wait to get to the port. I'm phoning the Medevac agency to arrange a suitable rendezvous point for the helicopter.'

'I'll get the Medevac checklist.'

Francesca started completing the essential checklist that would give the Medevac team all the vital information they needed to know about the patient. By the time she had finished Gabriel had put down the phone. He quickly checked Elena again, noting her BP and pulse and checking her IV fluids.

'Have you told her yet?' he asked.

Francesca shook her head. 'I wanted to wait until you had confirmed it with the captain. Do you want me to tell her now?'

Gabriel shook his head. 'Let me,' he said.

There it was again. Compassion for his patient. This from a man who had thrown her friend out on the street in the middle of the night. Some things just didn't add up. How long would it take Jill to answer that email?

He walked over to where Elena was lying and took her hand again. 'Elena? It's Dr Russo. I need to speak to you again.'

Her eyes flickered open at the sound of his voice. She was obviously still in pain.

'Elena, I think that the ectopic pregnancy has probably ruptured and caused bleeding into your abdomen. That's why you are feeling so unwell.' He pointed to the IV fluids hanging next to her. 'These can only help for a limited amount of time. You really need to have surgery to stop the bleeding.'

'But how can I?'

'We've made arrangements for you to be air-lifted off the ship and taken to a nearby hospital. The helicopter will be here soon, we just need to make sure you are ready to be moved.'

She looked shocked at the prospect and twisted uncomfortably on the bed, her face still racked with pain. 'But where will it land?'

Gabriel spoke reassuringly. 'Deck Sixteen—the sports deck has room for the helicopter to land next to the jogging track. We'll arrange to take you up there once we have word they will be arriving.'

The phone rang in the nearby office and Gabriel came out. 'The closest largest town with medical facilities is Amaliada. They have a large general hospital that can deal with this. We're around ninety miles off the coast from Amaliada right now. That was the captain. He's cleared the landing site and ETA is in the next ten minutes. We better get a move on.'

Francesca produced some thick woollen blankets to protect Elena from the wind and tucked them round her. Gabriel finished casting his eye over the Medevac checklist and signed it. He grabbed the nearest luminescent jacket and pulled it over his uniform; Francesca and Kevin were already wearing theirs. 'Are we good to go?' he checked, and when they nodded in agreement he released the brake on the trolley and started pushing it out of the door.

His hand and forearm were next to Francesca's and she glanced up at him, wondering if he realised his hand was touching hers. His head was down and he seemed totally focused on his task, then, out of the blue, he gave her hand a little squeeze and shot her a quick grin. Two other crew members were waiting in the corridor for them to clear the path to the nearest lift. Francesca watched Elena carefully. Her BP was still low and colour poor, but she could already hear the hum of the approaching helicopter so it wouldn't be long now.

The doors of the lift opened at Deck Sixteen and they were immediately met by the biting wind caused by the hovering helicopter. The noise was deafening.

'Let's stay in here until the helicopter lands,' shouted Gabriel. They watched as four crewman wearing luminescent jackets like their own, and carrying paddles, signalled the helicopter it was safe to land.

The helicopter touched down and they ran forward, pulling the trolley between them and keeping their heads down low. A Medevac team member opened the side door of the helicopter and jumped out.

'Dr Russo?' he shouted above the din of the rotating blades. Gabriel nodded and helped move Elena onto the helicopter's own trolley, which could be easily lifted inside. He bent his head next to the Medevac team member, handing over the checklist and shouting some extra instructions.

Francesca and Kevin pulled the medical centre trolley back towards the lift, moving out of the way of the crewmen who were ready to signal the helicopter to lift off.

Gabriel ran over to join them next to the lift and in a matter of seconds the door banged shut and the helicopter took off into the sky with a small wave from the Medevac team member. They watched as the noise dissipated and the whirring blades became a blur in the distance.

Silence fell over them. All that was left was the steady sound of the ship's engines, purring away in the dark of the night.

'Well,' said Gabriel, the serious expression leaving his face and a wicked glint in his brown eyes as he turned towards Francesca. He gave her a wink. 'A near drowning, a resuscitation and an ectopic pregnancy all in the space of one week. Who said this job was boring!'

CHAPTER FOUR

'DID you know about this?'

Gabriel looked distinctly unimpressed. He was holding the pink piece of paper containing the 'cougar list' in his hand. The tape was still stuck to the top of the page and the cupboard door was lying open.

She smiled. 'Oops. Did I forget to mention that?'

'Yes. You did.'

For a second she almost felt guilty. But it didn't last long. He was scowling at her again. The thrill and adrenaline from last night was gone and they were back to the routine of her hating him and him watching her every move. This would be a long day.

He was still growling at her. 'Any reason you didn't tell me about it?'

Because I think you're a snake and you deserved a bit of your own medicine.

The words danced around her brain. She bit her lip to stop herself from saying them out loud. Why did he look so mad? Offended almost?

Was he currently reading her less than complimentary thoughts?

She tried to change the subject quickly. 'It's probably going to be quiet today—most of the passengers will disembark at Piraeus to go on the sightseeing tours of Athens.' Francesca picked up a crew list. 'Katherine is working too this morning so it would probably be best if we tried to cover as many of the crew medicals as possible.'

Gabriel glanced over the list, underlining a few names in red. 'These are the ones I want to see.'

Francesca felt her lips tighten. The role of the advanced nurse practitioner was one that some doctors struggled to understand. Her job included most of the extended skills that general nurses could do—cannulation, suturing, venepuncture. But she also had advanced skills in reading X-rays, prescribing some general medications and diagnostic skills more equated with those of a junior doctor.

On a day-to-day basis these weren't always

needed. Most patients attended with minor illnesses, respiratory and gastrointestinal infections, minor skin complaints and fractures and accidental injuries that happened either on board or ashore.

But the crew medicals could involve more intensive work-ups and regular reviews of ongoing chronic conditions, and Francesca enjoyed doing them. Gabriel had just underlined some of the patients that she normally reviewed herself and it irked her.

'I normally see these patients.' She pointed to the few he'd marked on the list.

His brow narrowed. 'And today I'm going to see them.'

Was he just being pig-headed? Did he think this a role that only a doctor could fulfil? Or was he just doing this to annoy her?

'But I've seen these patients on a regular basis. I understand them, and how they deal with their conditions. Surely it would be best if they were reviewed by someone familiar with their set of circumstances?' She was determined to keep the annoyance out of her voice. She wanted to sound professional. She wanted to sound completely rational.

Gabriel seemed unmoved. 'Like I said, today I'm going to see them.' He picked up the list and started walking to his room. 'Sometimes it takes a fresh pair of eyes to look over a case to decide on the best plan of treatment for a patient.'

She could feel the hackles at the back of her neck rise.

She wanted to shout. She wanted to tell him he was condescending. She wanted to tell him to stop trying to find fault with her. Did he really think she was going to fall for that lame excuse?

She knew he was going to look over all her patient consult notes to see if he could find a reason to get rid of her. Did he have to be so obvious?

She turned and smiled sweetly, pasting a smile so sickly on to her face he would have no doubt what she was thinking. 'Whatever you think, Dr Russo.' She picked up her copy of the list and headed into the next room, sitting down in front of one of the computers and tapping furiously.

Her mind whirred. *I hate him. He's a superficial, condescending git. He has more money than sense. He flung Jill onto the street at 3:00 a.m. Who does that? How dared he? Does he think he can treat all women like that?*

'So what's with you and our hunky new Italian doctor? You can't keep your eyes off him.' Katherine had perched on the edge of the desk next to her.

'What?'

She smiled at Francesca and folded her arms. 'But I can't quite get what's going on between you two. When I say you can't keep your eyes off him—it's not in a good way. You look at him as if you're plotting fifty different ways to kill him and hide the body.' She shook her head knowingly. 'Now, that isn't the sweet-natured Francesca I know and love.' She bent across the desk, closing the space between them both and propping her chin on one hand. 'So what gives? Are you a lover scorned? Did you meet in a past life? Were you secret childhood sweethearts—?'

'Have you completely lost your mind?'

Katherine's face broke into a wide smile. She nodded her head, 'See? I knew it. I *knew* there was something there.' She couldn't hide the self-satisfied look from her face. 'So why do you hate him so much? Because, to be honest, after that one hellish night doing his neuro obs I've found him quite charming. And so has everyone else. And have you seen him with kids? The guy is *seriously* good with them.'

Francesca shook her head. She couldn't believe this. She couldn't believe the rest of the staff was fooled by his good looks and killer abs. She finished the notes she was inputting and turned to face Katherine.

'I think he's conceited. I feel as if he's constantly looking over my shoulder, trying to find fault.'

Katherine sighed. 'He's only been here just over a week. How can you possibly think that?'

Francesca held up the list. 'Look at this. He's taken all my usual crew members for review. He's checking up on me. He's trying to find fault.'

'Or maybe he's the new guy and he's trying to work out how we do things around here?'

Her words hung in the air. Francesca didn't like them. It made her look as if *she* was trying to find fault with him. Not the other way about.

'You honestly find him charming?'

Katherine nodded slowly, her gaze disappearing off into the distance. 'Yeah, he is kind of charming. And those dark brown eyes are just to die for. And his teeth…' She turned back to face Francesca. 'He's got a set of teeth that could appear in a television commercial. When I was doing his neuro obs in the middle of the night he got up for a shower. Now, that really was an eyeful.' She was off again, into her daydream-like state.

Francesca cringed. All the things that she'd noticed first about Gabriel. The kind of superficial things that shouldn't really matter. Looks were only skin deep. Words that she'd repeated over and over again to Jill.

And yet she'd done it herself. She'd seen him lying on the bottom of that boat and for a second had thought, Wow. Totally unprofessional. Thank goodness hearing his name had brought her back to her senses.

'Don't be fooled by his looks, Katherine. It's what's inside that counts. And I have it on good authority that his handsome looks don't penetrate beneath the surface.'

Katherine looked shocked. 'What does that mean?'

'He used to date one of my friends. And he didn't treat her particularly well.'

'Why, what happened?'

Francesca waved her hand. 'I don't want to get into it. Needless to say, the feelings are mutual. I'm not impressed to be working with him and he's not impressed to be working with me.' Francesca shook her head. 'And anyway, is it the handsome looks that are the attraction or is it the fact the man is practically dripping with diamonds?'

Katherine's pretty face turned into a frown. 'Now I really have no idea what you're talking about.'

'Gabriel Russo? Member of one of the richest families in Venice?'

Katherine shook her head. The name obviously meant nothing to her.

Francesca sighed and turned back to the computer, tapping into one of the internet search engines. 'I hadn't heard of him, either. But after he treated my friend so badly I looked him up. See?' She turned the screen to face Katherine.

Katherine leaned forward. 'Oh, wow!' Headline after headline. All about the Russo family and how they were one of the first printing families in Venice. Image after image appeared on the screen. Francesca drew in a sharp breath.

'What is it? Is it that one?' Katherine pointed to a brown, muscled, very well-endowed picture of Gabriel perched on the edge of a brilliant yacht in a pair of white swimming trunks. The picture left nothing to the imagination. It could have adorned the walls of teenage girls up and down the country.

'What? Yes… I mean, no.' Francesca sighed. 'That's my friend.' She pointed to a figure in the background of the picture, a young blonde in a turquoise bikini. 'I just didn't expect to see her online.'

Katherine read a few more of the headlines. 'It seems our new resident doc is dripping with diamonds. So what's he doing here?'

'It's a good question and I've no idea. I just know I won't be joining his fan club.'

'Look at that.'

'What?' Francesca really didn't want to look at another picture of Gabriel in his swim shorts.

But Katherine was pointing at some professional journal articles, all with Gabriel's name attached, and all on paediatrics. So he specialised in paediatrics. The penny dropped. That explained his actions the other day. That was why he was so good with kids. How come he hadn't mentioned it?

Katherine pursed her lips. 'So what's he like?'

'What do you mean—what's he like? It wasn't me who used to date him.'

'No, I mean as a doctor. You worked with him last night—and I heard you didn't tell him about the cougar list, by the way, naughty, naughty.' She waggled her finger at Francesca. 'Was he any good?'

Francesca almost felt the words stick in her throat. Last night *had* bothered her. Whilst she knew someone who was a rat in real life could be professionally good at their job, it was more than that. She'd seen the compassion in Gabriel's eyes when he'd spoken to their patient. He'd been more than calm and competent in a situation in which others might have panicked. Especially when he was new on board. Especially now that she knew his speciality was paediatrics. He could have felt totally out of his depth and how much help would she have given him?

'He was fine.' Struck by the realisation of how well he'd performed the night before, it was as much as she could manage.

The look on Katherine's face said it all as she slid off the desk. 'He was fine? He diagnosed an ectopic pregnancy and organised an emergency airlift—probably saving a life on his first night on call. All from a guy who specialises in paediatrics, and "he was fine"?' She nodded her head sarcastically and disappeared out of the room.

Francesca felt overwhelmed. So much had happened in the last few days. She couldn't make sense of most of it. Most of the time she couldn't stand to be around Gabriel. But even that confused her. Everyone else thought he was charming, so why couldn't she?

It would be easy to say it was her extended knowledge of him. But there was something else. Something she hated.

The way she found her eyes following him around the room.

The way she believed the compassion in his eyes the night before had been real.

The admiration she'd felt for his skill while treating Elena.

The fact that if this was another life, another set of circumstances, she might actually be attracted to him.

A sense of loneliness swept over her, coupled with the feelings of inadequacy creeping up out of nowhere. The feeling of being under a microscope, her every move examined. Completely exposed.

She thought back to last night—automatically falling into self-preservation mode. She'd been right about Elena's condition. She'd made the right call. A new feeling of determination swept over her. Her mind was telling her one thing but her churning stomach telling her another. Why did she feel so unsure?

Katherine's words echoed in her brain. *He diagnosed an ectopic pregnancy and organised an emergency airlift—probably saving a life on his first night on call.*

Francesca was left staring at her screen. 'I diagnosed the ectopic pregnancy,' she whispered to the empty room.

* * *

Gabriel was furious. He'd gone back to raise a query with Francesca about a patient's medication and he'd caught the words 'dripping with diamonds'. They'd sent an icy chill down his spine.

He hadn't listened to much more—he didn't need to. Once more he'd been judged and valued on his bank balance rather than his clinical expertise.

He hated internet search engines with a passion. Wasn't a person allowed a modicum of privacy any more?

So now he was being judged on his money once again. His family name. How long before they found the word 'tragedy' attached to something and started to tiptoe round about him?

It was the overwhelming reason he'd chosen to work overseas—away from Italy and its close-knit gentry. Away from others who were aware of his family background.

It was bad enough that she hadn't told him about the cougar list. Yet another person sitting in judgement of him and believing the gossip.

For a second—just for a second last night—

he'd seen a glimmer of hope in Francesca. She'd seemed an able and competent nurse. More than that, she'd shown good instincts. Even if she hadn't been sure of them herself, they had still been there. It would have been so easy for her not to ask for a consultation on their patient.

Some medical staff would have been content with the endometriosis diagnosis and assumed that some of the cells had spread, causing more pain and inflammation. Most would probably have given a stronger painkiller with instructions to come back if there was no improvement.

Might he have done that?

Last night he'd had respect for his prickly nurse—despite her poor choice of friend. Respect because she'd earned it.

Today she was back in the doldrums of disgust. Francesca had already told him she knew who he was and questioned his need to work. To earn his own salary.

But she knew nothing about his attempts to distance himself from the family business. About the general chaos he'd created as a teenager when he'd announced his intentions not to move into the well-paid position created for him but to follow the career of his heart. The one imprinted into his being years before.

He was the last remaining son—his father had been devastated by his decision. But Gabriel had been determined—nothing would change his mind. And his strong, intelligent and often overlooked sister was more than ready to step into his shoes, with a passion, drive and commitment to the family business that Gabriel could never have equalled.

Francesca knew none of this and probably would never understand. Not if she had the same mindset as her friend. One that could never look underneath the surface.

Jill had been horrified when she'd been caught with Gabriel's twenty-thousand-pound watch stuffed in her bag. He might have even believed the feeble story she'd started to spout if he hadn't seen her deliberately take it and hide it in the inside pocket. She was lucky he'd only flung her out on the street instead of calling the police.

Why did Francesca feel the need to tell all her colleagues about his wealth? He'd hoped to be part of a team that would judge him on his clinical competence, not the fact he was 'dripping with diamonds'.

How could he trust anyone now? Rich kids learned quickly that wealth attracted all sorts of insincere friends. It had never really been an issue at work before.

And now Francesca had made it an issue by gossiping.

He gritted his teeth. He wanted to hate her—he really did.

But he'd noticed something. Her happy, bubbly exterior with her colleagues was just that—an exterior. Scratch the surface and who knew what he might find? There had been a wistfulness in her eyes that had looked as if it reached down into her very soul. She genuinely hadn't trusted her instincts last night and he had to wonder why. She was a good nurse. She should have confidence in her abilities. Had something or someone taken her confidence away?

Whether he liked it or not, she was part of this team.

He wanted to work with competent, confident individuals. He liked to know their strengths—and their weaknesses—to get the best possible results for the patients they were serving. Here things would be no different.

It was why he'd taken some of her patients today. She seemed an able and competent nurse but he wanted to dig a little deeper.

So far, he'd found nothing to concern him. All the patients she'd seen had been well cared for. Her decisionmaking was sound. In fact, what he'd seen had given him even more confidence in her abilities.

Not that she'd ever know. She'd looked as if she was going to bite him when he'd said he wanted to check over her patients.

As a doctor he nearly always had staff to mentor, opportunities to increase their learning experience and instil confidence in their abilities. He just hadn't expected to find it here on a cruise ship. He'd almost expected the rest of the staff to be running circles around about him based on their longer experience. But it wasn't the case with Francesca. And whether he liked her or not, he was determined to find out why.

CHAPTER FIVE

ONE week later Francesca felt as if she was still fighting to see her own patients. Gabriel had reviewed practically every staff member she'd ever seen. And for a man who'd spent the last six years in paediatrics he was a meticulous adult practitioner who missed nothing.

If she hadn't been so busy she would have been nervous. What if he did find something wrong? What if she'd mismanaged a patient?

Working with Gabriel was like walking a tightrope. Constantly teetering on the high wire, with him waiting to see her fall. There was no doubt he wouldn't be there to catch her. It was almost a certainty that he'd watch her splat on the ground like some fly on a windscreen.

He was constantly looking over her shoulder, asking her seemingly inane work-related questions. She was sure he was trying to catch her out and she felt like an amoeba under a microscope.

She almost wished he'd just come out and tell her that, rather than pussyfoot round about her. She preferred the direct approach rather than the wolf in sheep's clothing.

Everyone else around him was well and truly smitten. With the rest of the staff and the passengers, his Italian charm served him well. But the air between the two of them still crackled with animosity.

Francesca hated to admit it but there was something really intimidating about an insanely handsome man hating the ground you walked on. Sometimes she caught him looking at her with a strange expression on her face, as if he was trying to get the measure of her. She'd no idea why.

He could the see the practical examples of her work all over the ship. He could audit her written and electronic records until he was blue in the face. She was almost sure there was nothing for him to find.

But it was that little touch of uncertainty that made her nervous. No matter how well she performed there was almost always a tiny part of her wondering if she'd missed something. Wondering if she was about to make a mistake that would affect someone's life.

Before her father's death it had never been there. She'd been confident at her work and in her abilities. But no matter how hard she tried, she felt as if that confidence would never return.

It was always going to be there—that little voice in her head, telling her to guard herself and walk carefully. Questioning her abilities. Just the way Gabriel was constantly doing.

And worse still it was all her own fault.

There was nobody else to blame.

She'd allowed herself to be swept off her feet by a playboy doc just like Gabriel. A man with the attention span of a goldfish and the staying power of an ice cream on a sunny day.

But for a few months she'd been smitten. More important, she'd been distracted.

She'd spent less time with her father, too busy being swept from one date to the next by Dr Wonderful. Except he wasn't.

If only she'd paid attention. If only she'd spotted the signs of what her father had been planning. But she hadn't.

Now she had to live with the consequences. And Dr Wonderful? All the more reason to stay away from men like Gabriel. Turned out he hadn't been so wonderful after all. He'd dropped her like a hot brick when her father had died. Thank goodness for Jill.

How long could she work in this environment?

And what had happened to her Australian visa?

She looked down at the two lists in front of her—one for crew, one for passengers. Finally, a patient of her own to review. For a second she almost felt relief that he wasn't checking up on her today, then a glance at the passenger list made her realise that four children were waiting to be seen.

Gabriel always wanted to see the children himself. It was natural—he was a paediatrician after all. But he was almost a little too fastidious about it. To the point of being slightly obsessional. He'd even asked David Marsh to page him, whether he was on duty or not, to see any children requiring treatment.

Maybe the man was just a control freak. But she hadn't noticed it in anything else that he did. And it hadn't been on the list of complaints from Jill, either.

Jill. She still hadn't emailed Francesca back yet and Francesca was curious to know what her response would be. She couldn't quite decide whether Jill would send a rant about what a louse Gabriel was or a request for new pictures of her unrequited love. You could never tell with that girl.

Francesca gave a sigh and picked up the crew list. It was time to do some work. The waiting room already had a few customers.

'Roberto Franc, please.' Francesca smiled and ushered him into a nearby consulting room.

Roberto Franc was a twenty-year-old busboy on the ship. He had been diagnosed with diabetes mellitus a few weeks before and was struggling to control his condition. Diabetes mellitus was usually diagnosed in childhood and Roberto was older than the average new patient but Francesca was confident she could help him cope.

He settled into the chair opposite Francesca, pushing his diary across the desk towards her.

'How are you?' she asked.

'Not bad,' he muttered. She took the diary from him and glanced at its contents. Newly diagnosed diabetics were taught to monitor their blood-sugar results regularly and record them in a diary. It helped give an accurate picture of how they were coping on insulin injections, and if the injections were controlling their blood sugars accordingly.

'I can see you've been testing frequently,' Francesca said. 'Sometimes six times a day—how are your fingers?'

'Sore.' He lifted his hands and placed them palms upward on the desk in front of her.

She could see the little marks on his fingertips where the tiny lancet had pierced his fingers. The little dots appeared all over his fingertips, with some fingers looking slightly swollen. 'I think we can help with that,' she said. 'What type of meter do you have?'

He pulled a black package from the back pocket of his trousers. It was little bigger than a wallet, but when opened contained his testing strips, blood glucose meter and lancet holder. Francesca smiled, recognising the type of meter.

She pulled the instruction card from inside the front pocket. 'I know it's hard initially, but until we have your blood sugars completely under control it is important that you keep testing. There are other sites you can take blood from—it doesn't always have to be from your fingertips.' She showed him on the instruction leaflet. 'You could try the forearm.'

He nodded slowly. 'I hadn't really thought of that.'

'It would give your fingers a few days to recover—you might find it useful to try.' She was still studying his diary carefully. 'I think we need to adjust some of your insulin doses,' she continued slowly. 'Your injection that you take at night—the long-lasting insulin that gives you a backdrop throughout the day—it needs to go up a little.' She pointed at the diary 'For the last week your blood-sugar levels have been quite high in the mornings when you wake up, that tells us we need to adjust the insulin you take last thing at night. We will put it up by two units initially and review it again in another week.'

He nodded thoughtfully. 'What about the dinnertime dose?'

'I notice that you've had a few hypoglycaemic attacks around 7:00 p.m. When have you been having lunch?'

'About three o'clock, after all the passengers have finished.' Francesca was aware that as a busboy Roberto would be expected to be on duty during lunch and dinner service times. It made it more difficult to control his own eating times. He wouldn't be having lunch till three and dinner till around nine. Hypos—or hypoglycaemic attacks—happened when a person's blood sugar fell too low. It didn't just affect people with diabetes. Lots of people could become tired, lack concentration or become cranky if they didn't eat for a while and, as a result, their blood sugar became low. For Roberto however, it was more serious. Diabetics' blood-sugar levels could fall so low that they could lose consciousness.

'How did you feel when you had the hypos? Did you have any warning signs?'

Roberto raised his hands and shrugged his shoulders. 'On a few occasions I was trembling and sweaty, and at those times I knew to sit down and have something to eat. On other occasions I haven't noticed so much, especially when it's busy during service. I dropped some plates the other night and one of the other bus-boys came and told me to sit down as I was a terrible colour. I checked my blood sugar then and it was low.'

'Okay.' Francesca nodded reassuringly. 'It takes time to recognise the signs of a hypogly-caemic attack—and they can be different in every person with diabetes. I realise it's even more difficult if you're busy and thinking about other things. It's good that your colleagues know what is wrong with you and can point out if you're not looking so good.'

His face twisted in frustration. 'But I hate that. I want to be able to control this myself.'

'I know all about how frustrating diabetes is. My dad was diabetic for years. Sometimes he struggled to control it, too. You've just been di-agnosed and you need to give it a little time.' She patted his hand. 'We will get this under con-trol. I think you need to reduce the insulin dose you're taking at three o'clock when you're hav-ing your lunch. It's a short-acting insulin and could be contributing to the hypos you've been having around 7:00 p.m. It could still be lasting in your body, particularly if you haven't eaten enough, or if your physical activity levels have been raised.

'We'll reduce it just by a few units, two would be best. I would also suggest that you need to have a think about how long you go between meals. I think you should have an extra snack around six. It's a long time until nine when you actually eat your evening meal.'

'But that's right when service starts for evening meals so we're really busy then.'

'I know that. But if you eat just before the doors open at six o'clock, then you'll probably be fine throughout service. I can speak to the dining room manager if it helps.'

'Thanks, you'll probably have to. I don't want him to think I'm shirking off.'

Francesca made a little note in his file. 'That's no problem. I'll speak to him today. Keep doing your blood-sugar readings and make the adjustments to your insulin as we've discussed. I've written a little note of them inside your diary. I'll give you an appointment for the same time next week and we'll see how you're doing.'

Roberto stood up from his chair and put his

diary and meter back in his pockets. 'That's great, thanks, Nurse Cruz.'

'My pleasure.'

She showed him out to the door, and then headed back to put some more notes in his file and record his appointment in the book for next week.

Gabriel was standing at the doorway, his arms folded across his chest, watching her intently. He'd obviously finished seeing his four children in record time.

'That's quite a gift you've got.'

Her head snapped up from the appointment book. She realised that he must have been listening to her from the consulting-room door. She had been so focused on her patient that she hadn't noticed. A pink tinge of embarrassment flushed her cheeks. 'What do you mean?'

'You dealt with him like a real expert—as if you really understood.'

She could feel the adrenaline cursing through her veins. *Fight or flight syndrome.* Gabriel was being nice to her—should she be suspicious right now or not? 'I do.'

'So I gathered. How long was your dad diabetic?'

'From around the same age. He was actually really well controlled, but I grew up recognising any signs of hypo in him and knew how to deal with it. Later in life, when things were a little more difficult for him, I helped adjust his insulin when he needed it.'

'It must have been a distinct advantage, having a daughter who was a nurse.'

Francesca shook her head and he could almost see her cringe. 'To be honest, most of the things I learned about diabetes I already knew before I started my nursing. But it made it easier for me when looking after patients with diabetes, and for dealing with the families.'

'You seemed to cover everything. Even how he must be feeling and coping with his fears and anxieties. You're good.'

It was a compliment but as soon as he'd said the words a shadow passed over her face. 'Not that good.' The words were quiet, almost whispered.

'What?'

He sensed her take a deep breath and saw her

straighten, pushing her shoulders back. 'All nurses are supposed to practice holistic care,' she said, as if she was quoting straight from a textbook. 'But don't kid yourself. I'm not a mental health nurse. Experience has taught me I'm not good at any of that kind of stuff.'

Gabriel stopped his mouth from automatically opening in response. It would be so easy to pursue this. It would be so easy to ask her exactly what she meant by that. But Gabriel didn't pry. If she wanted to tell him she would. Was this the reason she had no confidence at work?

She tried to change the subject quickly to deflect what was obviously on his mind. 'I guess you could say diabetes was one of my "babies". We all have them. What's yours?'

'Paediatrics. It was the only reason I came into medicine. I always wanted to work with children.'

She tilted her head to the side. 'But yet you don't have any of your own. Makes me wonder about you, Gabriel. Too much playboy, not enough family man. Maybe it's time for you to settle down.' He had no idea how relieved she was right now to have moved the conversation away from her dad. The one person she didn't want to talk about. Not to anyone.

But Gabriel didn't look too happy now. His relaxed expression had disappeared. 'Having children has never been high on my agenda. Taking care of children has.'

There was finality in his words. Determination.

She wanted to reply, *But you've ended up on a cruise ship,* but the words stuck in her throat. Something told her not to respond that way. Not right now.

Katherine appeared at the door, her face pale and her hands on her stomach. It broke the instant tension in the room. He walked straight over and put his arm around her shoulders. 'What's wrong?'

'I'm not feeling so good.' She glanced between them. 'Do either of you mind if I go and lie down for a few hours?'

Francesca shook her head and Gabriel guided Katherine towards the door. 'Of course not. The clinics are finished for this morning and it's only emergency callouts this afternoon. Francesca and I can manage those. Go and lie down. And give me a page if you need anything.' He nodded at Francesca, who smiled in response.

'Thanks, you two. See you later.' Katherine practically bolted out the door.

Francesca bit her lip. 'Please let this be just an upset stomach. The last thing we need is a Norovirus outbreak.'

Gabriel's brow wrinkled as the realisation of her words hit him. There had been several cruise ships last year that had been affected by Norovirus. Cruises had had to be stopped and vessels berthed and deep-cleaned or sanitised before any new trips were started. It had been a nightmare for both crew and passengers.

He groaned. 'I hadn't even thought of that.' He shot her a quick smile as he leaned back in his chair. 'A Medevac, a near drowning and now a possible outbreak. I'm turning into the bad-luck fairy, aren't I?'

Francesca shook her head. 'There are always a few people aboard that become unwell. Katherine could just be unlucky. The next few hours will tell us if we need to put our public health hats on. Let's cross our fingers that we don't.'

She walked over to the side of the room, her

eyes resting on a calendar in front of her. A tight fist was clenched around her heart as she realised the date. She felt physically sick. Almost instantly tears formed in her eyes. Was it the seventeenth already? How could she not have noticed?

She turned quickly to Gabriel. 'If you don't need me, I'm going up on deck to catch a little sun.' Before he had a chance to answer, she was gone.

Gabriel leaned back in his chair. For once the medical centre was empty.

He felt frustrated. Just when he thought he might have had an opportunity to talk to Francesca. To try and dig a little deeper, to try and find out what was going on in her head. But she'd dashed out of here like a startled rabbit.

He was sure she'd brushed a tear from her face as she'd left out the room. What on earth was wrong with her?

Should he go after her?

He looked around him, trying to figure out why. What on earth could have made her cry?

Nothing stood out. The conversation about Norovirus had been totally work related and entirely unremarkable. There was no reason for her reaction.

He was torn. The last thing he wanted to do was unintentionally upset another member of staff, even if the atmosphere between them had been prickly. Even if her actions at times had annoyed him.

He'd tried to brush aside the playboy comments. He didn't want to go down that road. What was the point in finding a wife and settling down? He'd seen what happened to families. There were some things that you could never recover from.

And although he'd never courted the media, being labelled a playboy wasn't so bad. It meant that most women had no illusions about him. No expectations.

His father had been furious at his decision to become a doctor. The printing business was their legacy, their mark on the world. Who was going to continue that now?

The reminder that Gabriel was the last remaining male was clear and it had stung. He could still picture his father's face—red with anger and glistening with sweat.

But even as a teenager Gabriel had been clear that saving lives was more important than a family business. Saving lives like Dante's. Surely his father had to be rational? Had to see the reasoning behind Gabriel's decision?

He'd dismissed him with the wave of a hand. And Gabriel had been furious with his father— at his lack of acknowledgement of Dante's lost life. At the way he'd focused on his work instead of his family, causing Gabriel to step into his shoes at far too young an age.

And now, with his increased frailty, it was happening again.

He looked over at the clock, calculating the time difference between Greece and Italy. He had an ideal opportunity to sort out of some of his father's day-to-day work duties. He could put this time to good use and maybe even fit in a phone call to find out how his father was feeling.

Whatever was wrong with Francesca would have to wait—even though it did leave his stomach churning.

He really didn't have time to waste on some nurse.

CHAPTER SIX

FRANCESCA was feeling sick and it was nothing to do with a bug. She dashed along the corridor to her cabin. How could she not have noticed the date?

Eighteen months ago today. Eighteen months since her father had committed suicide and she'd found his body sitting in the armchair in his house, with a letter for her and a bottle of pills next to it.

It didn't matter where she was, or what she was doing. The seventeenth of the month was always a day where she felt in the doldrums. It was always a day she needed to clear her head.

It was also a day that was usually imprinted on her brain. What had happened to her?

She threw off her uniform and pulled on her swimming costume and matching red sarong. She needed to be out in the fresh air as the walls seemed to be closing in on her.

A few minutes later she reached the adults-only part of the ship. Away from the frantic swimming pools and happy families crowded onto sun loungers.

Up here in the adults-only section there were wicker pod sun loungers, the cocooned structures designed to give a little more comfort and a little shelter from the sun's rays. She flopped down into one and pulled her book from her bag.

There was a fantastic view of the sea from here. The beautiful blue sea that stretched on for miles and miles. The sun's rays licked at her toes and she could feel the cooling sea breezes through her hair. She always escaped up here when she needed to. The ship was huge, but still a confined environment, and it was often hard to get some time and space on your own.

She stared out ahead. The tears already prickling at her eyes. Why hadn't she noticed? Why hadn't she realised just how bad her dad had been feeling?

He'd taken the loss of her mum really hard. But that had been five years before and after a dark spell of depression he'd seemed to be making improvements. He'd started to go out more, eat a little better and socialise with friends again.

It was probably why she'd felt safe enough to allow distractions. To listen to the insincere words of flattery from the playboy doc and be fooled by them.

Her father's suicide had been like an absolute bolt from the blue.

And his handwritten letter had just broken her heart.

He couldn't face life any more without his beloved wife. And as much as he loved Francesca, he felt as if he was holding her back. It was time to go.

Did he think she'd found someone to love?

She'd taken a job back in Glasgow after her mum had died as she hadn't wanted to leave her dad on his own. The truth was, she *had* turned down other job opportunities so she could stay in Glasgow with her dad, but she'd never mentioned them. And after he was gone she'd flitted from job to job, gaining experience and building her portfolio.

But nowhere had felt like home. Nowhere had removed the ache of loneliness she always felt.

She closed her eyes. The padding inside the pod was wonderfully comfortable. The quiet sound of the sea was calming. The book slipped from her hands.

'So this is where you've been hiding. There's good news and there's bad news. What do you want first?'

There was a jolt as the weight of someone sitting at the entrance of her pod made the whole structure move. Gabriel's voice broke into her dream. A dream of her father reading her favourite bedtime stories, Rapunzel, Cinderella.

For an instant she wanted to be angry with him. But the truth was she was getting used to him. Gabriel Russo wasn't turning out to be the man she'd thought he was. The more she saw of him the less deplorable he became.

She groaned. 'You've just ruined my dream.'

He leaned forward, his body entering into the pod. It seemed like an intimate gesture and she pushed herself further back into the cushions.

'Was it a good dream?'

'It was perfect.'

'Was I in it?' He'd switched on his million-dollar smile. There was no way she was going to be affected by it.

'Not a chance.'

Other women would love this. A sheltered pod on a huge cruise ship with a handsome man. His face was only inches away from hers, his body seemed even closer. Whilst her red swimming costume and sarong were normal attire for most of the passengers, she automatically wanted to cover herself up. He had a pair of beach shorts on and those killer abs were visible again. Why couldn't he put them away around her?

She pushed herself up a little, moving her legs closer to the pod entrance, the only route of escape. 'If you'd been in it Prince Charming would have turned into a slimy frog.'

'Ouch.' He sat up next to her at the pod entrance. 'What are you doing here?'

'I would have thought that was obvious. I'm being extremely lazy and lying here, reading a book.'

'What are you reading? Something pink and fluffy?'

She raised her eyebrows at him.

'Or something, dark, dangerous and mysterious?'

'What do you care?'

'I'm interested. I like to know what people read.' He picked up her book and looked at the title, flipping it over and starting to read the back cover blurb.

A smile crept across her face as she waited and watched for the penny to drop. Any second now his face would go scarlet and he would drop the book as if it were on fire.

But no. Nothing. Just the tiniest twitch of his leg. He turned and handed it back to her.

She knew exactly what part of the body a blurb like that would have an effect on.

His face remained calm. 'So, hot and sexy, then?'

She nodded, 'Yeah, definitely hot and sexy.' She raised an eyebrow at him. 'A girl can dream, right?'

What was she doing? She'd just flirted with him. The man she hated. The man who was watching her every move. Was she mad?

Gabriel's dark brown eyes were getting even

darker. He sat up straighter. 'About tonight...' he started.

'What about tonight? I'm off duty.'

'Yeah, I know.' He shrugged his shoulders. 'But Katherine's feeling really bad. She wondered if you'd mind covering for her.'

'Is that the good news or the bad news?'

'It depends entirely what you think of the next bit. Katherine was supposed to be on dining-room duty tonight, eating with some of the passengers.'

Francesca nodded. 'Yeah, that's fine. What else?' All officers on the ship had to take a turn in dining with the passengers.

Gabriel smiled. 'I'm on that duty, too.'

Francesca groaned and flopped back inside the pod. 'Am I ever going to get rid of you?'

The words were there but the atmosphere between them had changed. There wasn't the same tension. There wasn't the same angst. It was almost as if they'd reached a mutual plateau.

'You owe me.'

She narrowed her eyes at him. 'What?'

He shook his head at her. 'You know well that after the dinner we're supposed to go and watch the entertainment—be a visible presence amongst the passengers without officially being on duty.'

'And so?' The cogs in her brain were starting to turn. Dining-room duty was easy—eat dinner, make general conversation with the passengers.

After that she would be free to have a few drinks. She wouldn't be expected to respond to any patient queries—Kevin and David were on duty for those—so she could let her hair down. Try and forget about this bad day.

'There's no way I'm going out there alone. You'll have to watch the entertainment with me. You can rescue me from any cougars that may be about. You know—the ones you forgot to tell me about.'

She started to laugh and pushed herself up from the entrance to the pod. 'But you deserved that.' She lifted her book and pressed it close to her chest. 'As a professional courtesy I might agree to stay in your company.' She rolled her eyes at him. 'I'd hate it if our ship's doctor got caught in a compromising position.'

She turned to leave. 'But in that case it will

cost you. I'm planning on having a few drinks tonight—and you're buying. See ya.' Francesca sashayed her way across the desk. She could almost feel his eyes burning a hole into her spine. One sentence at the forefront of her brain.

What on earth are you doing, Fran?

Francesca had managed to smile and nod her way through the eight p.m. dinner even though she hadn't been able to eat a bite. Her eyes had watched every minute tick past on the clock in the dining room.

Gabriel had been seated with a family at the table next to hers. Her eyes had kept straying in his direction and she'd watch him read *The Cat in the Hat* to one of the young kids as the adults ate their dinner.

He'd seemed totally at ease and relaxed sitting amongst the family. She'd even heard him laugh. Was that possible for Gabriel?

It was obvious why he was a paediatrician. He was great with kids, had a real affinity with them. It made her wonder why he didn't have any of his own.

This afternoon had been the most relaxed she'd seen him since he'd got here. He hadn't been staring at her with those disapproving eyes.

Maybe they were both tiring of the constant prickliness between them. The jagged edges that had been clashing together were finally being worn down. To be replaced by…what?

Because there was still something that crackled in the air between them. The animosity had been replaced by something else. An underlying current that had been there since they'd first met. That neither of them had acknowledged or acted on. Until now.

The tension had built inside her so much that it was a relief when dinner finally finished at nine p.m. and she was able to make her excuses and rush back to her cabin.

Her laptop pinged behind her and she pressed the button. An email.

From Jill.

Her hand hesitated over the keyboard. What did she want this email to say? That she was furious that Gabriel was there, and rant about how badly he'd treated her? Or something else entirely? The *do I have a chance of getting back in there* type email. You could never tell which way Jill was going to go.

She pressed the button, her eyes automatically skimming the page.

Hi honey!

Gabriel Russo—well there's a blast from the past! Is he still as dashing and gorgeous than ever? No, don't answer that. I might be tempted again.

What on earth happened? Why did you have to resuscitate him? Can't imagine someone as fit as Gabriel falling overboard, so there must be more to it than that. Do tell.

I'd love the thought of being trapped in an enclosed space with him. I'm sure I could find a way to while away the hours with Dr Delicious. Tell him hi from me.

Have to go. Meeting Ferdinand for lunch. He's a duke or something.

Try not to fall out with Gabriel on my account— he was really just another notch on my bedpost. Send me some pictures of him if you can. And remember to tell me all the details!

Love Jill xx

Francesca didn't know whether to breathe a sigh of relief or throw up her hands in frustration. *'Tell him hi from me.'* What was that supposed to mean? And if Jill wasn't in the least perturbed at her working with Gabriel, why was she so bothered?

She slammed the laptop shut. It had taken Jill over two weeks to answer her email. She could wait for a response.

She wrinkled her nose. What exactly had Jill told her about Gabriel? Now she thought back to that night, not a lot. Was there a chance she might have misjudged Gabriel? Maybe she should lower her defences—just a little—and give him a chance to be friends?

Her fingers were trembling as she unfastened her dress uniform and hung it carelessly back in the cupboard. She grabbed the nearest dress, navy blue, stared at it and then flung it back. For some reason she didn't want something boring and dull. Gabriel was a gorgeous man. She didn't want people to glance over thinking, *What's he doing with her?*

Something had changed in her brain. She pulled out a red dress that she'd bought for New

Year; it was cut with a generous V-neckline to reveal her cleavage, and skirted just above her knees to show off her long legs. It sparkled with randomly placed sequins that added a little glamour to the colour of the dress. Francesca knew this dress showed off her curves well. Fashion rules said that you either revealed cleavage or legs but this dress made its own rules and showed a little of both—giving just a hint of what was underneath.

She picked up the gold filigree necklace she had bought in Venice a few months ago. It was the most expensive piece of jewellery that she owned—a gift to herself one year after her dad's funeral. He'd left her a little nest egg along with another amount that had instructions to buy something she would love for ever. So she'd wanted to buy something precious, something she could keep and remember him by.

She'd never really embraced her origins so an Italian necklace had seemed entirely appropriate. And somehow she knew he would approve. Especially today.

With its tiny beads of red murano glass it would go perfectly. She fastened the clasp around her neck. No other jewellery was necessary; the necklace was more than enough. She finished off her outfit with gold sandals and ran a quick brush through her chestnut locks. A flick of mascara and some ruby-coloured lipstick and she was ready. A glimpse out of the corner of her eye confirmed it was ten o'clock. A final squirt of perfume and she picked up her cabin card and left.

Gabriel was waiting in the Atlantis Bar. His brain was not entirely sure what he was doing there. Being one of the ship's doctors meant additional roles and responsibilities and he understood that. He'd invited Francesca merely as a means of self-protection. And if he kept telling himself that, he might actually grow to believe it. He eyed his watch nervously—what if she changed her mind and didn't come? The cougars were already circulating.

He looked at the drinks sitting on the bar. He had no idea what she drank, hadn't even thought to ask her beforehand, so he had thrown caution to the wind and decided to order something frivolous.

Seconds later he caught the scent of her perfume. He was standing facing the main entrance, but she must have came in via the side entrance and crept up behind him. His head swam with the sensual fusion of woody, amber and floral essences with hints of orange blossom. He turned swiftly to find her standing directly behind him.

'Is this mine?' She picked up one of the cocktail glasses sitting on the bar and without waiting for an answer put her lips to the edge of the glass and took a sip. Gabriel stood transfixed, moving his gaze from her deep brown eyes to her ruby-coloured lips sipping from the glass, finally catching a sparkle of the intricate gold creation around her neck.

'Gabriel?'

Her face had broken into a wild smile. 'Don't tell me I've just stolen someone else's drink from the bar?'

He snapped out of his daze. 'Yes. Of course it's yours—I just wasn't sure what to order.'

But it was the gold filigree necklace that attracted his attention most. He recognised the design and the workmanship of the piece.

The necklace was a piece of art. A piece of art

that he knew the value of. He was more than a little curious about who'd bought it for her.

Another little mystery about the woman who spoke so little about herself.

That afternoon he'd actually started to quite like her. He'd thought they might manage to have a working relationship. The tension between them seemed to have disintegrated and things had seemed almost manageable.

The sight of Francesca in her red swimsuit and sarong had sent blood rushing to parts of his body. As for her taste in books…

He felt as if he was finally getting to know her a little. Finally scratching beneath her prickly surface.

But what now?

Another thought started to creep into his brain. Francesca hadn't mentioned a lover or a boyfriend. She didn't wear any rings. Did she have some sugar daddy who had given her such an expensive present?

'Gabriel, what's wrong?'

She was standing directly under his nose. Her cocktail glass already empty, her dark brown eyes staring up at him. 'You've got the permanent frown on your face again.' She shot a beaming smile at a passenger who said hello on the way past. 'Can't you lighten up a bit?' she muttered. 'This is going to be a long evening.' She waved her cocktail glass at him. 'And I'm going to need another of these. What is it anyway?'

She was positioned right under his nose. And as he looked downwards his eyes were drawn directly to her deep cleavage. She was a knockout in that dress. Not that he hadn't noticed she was a knockout anyway but he'd been too busy disapproving of her to step back and take a good look.

But she seemed on edge, jittery almost. She'd drunk that cocktail in two minutes flat. What was her story? The other team members were open about their home lives, sharing photos and tales of their families and friends. But Francesca remained tight-lipped. He hardly knew a thing about her. What made her tick?

Her nursing skills were impeccable. He'd reviewed every case she'd worked on, observed her, spoken to staff and crew alike—Francesca didn't have a thing to worry about. So why was she nervous?

The intricate goldwork and highly polished murano glass of her necklace were shimmering under the neon lights of the Atlantis Bar. When she turned in certain directions the reflected light shone back on her face. And she was certainly attracting attention. If Gabriel had felt under scrutiny from the cougars earlier, it was nothing compared to the male reaction in the room to Francesca.

And she hadn't noticed. She flung back her head and laughed at something the man next to her said, her dark lustrous curls tossed over her shoulder. Her clingy red dress hugged her figure to perfection and the man had certainly noticed.

Gabriel was annoyed. He was *more* than annoyed. That guy should back off. Didn't he see that she was here with him?

He reached over and touched the necklace, circling his fingers around the droplet of red murano glass that skirted her cleavage. It might be a little forward but, hopefully, it would get rid of the man on the right.

'This is beautiful, Francesca. Where did you get it? Did a secret admirer buy it for you?'

Everything stopped. She'd been acutely conscious of standing next to him but not quite touching. Aware of his tall, broad frame and penetrating dark eyes. With his permanently knotted brow it was obvious that something was bothering him. He ought to be careful—if the wind changed his face could stay that way for ever. After watching him in the dining room to-night, she was beginning to think his frown was reserved solely for her.

Her eyes flickered up and down his body. He had changed from his dress uniform into dark trousers, a pale blue shirt and dark Italian shoes. It looked simple enough but was obviously expensive. Her eyes caught the several dark curled hairs revealed at the base of his throat. His Mediterranean skin was bronzed and alluring and his obvious muscled and well-proportioned body seemed to be attracting the attention of much of the female company in the room.

But he was with her.

And she'd been desperately trying to put that out of her mind.

And then he'd touched her, those fingertips unexpectedly brushing the swell of her breasts. Francesca froze. His fingers were fastened around the biggest piece of glass on her necklace and he was watching her. Waiting for an answer. Why couldn't she speak?

She shifted her weight on her feet. Right now she felt like a starstruck teenager. But why? She didn't even like this man so why on earth was he having this effect on her?

Maybe it was the email from Jill. It was strange that she hadn't made any derogatory comments about him. She hadn't been outraged at all. More interested in the details. All of it sent tiny alarm bells ringing in Francesca's head.

Maybe she had misjudged him? What would Gabriel say if she told him? Would he get that disapproving look on his face at the mention of Jill's name? Why was that? He was the one in the wrong.

Her stomach twisted, loyalty to Jill unsettling her.

His dark brown eyes were still staring at her. Watching every expression on her face. Did he know what she was thinking?

She really didn't want to explain about the necklace. She didn't want to tell him that her dad had left her money—that would take the conversation down a road she wasn't prepared to go.

He'd ask her how her father had died. It was only natural. And she didn't want to tell him about the suicide, particularly today—it was just too hard.

Then she'd have to admit she'd missed the signs and that if she'd paid more attention her beloved father might still be here.

Tonight her ambition was to drink herself into oblivion. And these strawberry-type cocktails were a good start. She had to steer this conversation away from the necklace as quickly as possible.

She gulped, struggling to find some words. 'Not so much a secret admirer,' she finally managed.

'No?'

His hand pulled her a little closer, the full length of her body coming into contact with his. What was he doing? She couldn't concentrate. 'I picked it myself. But it was a gift—to remind me of someone very dear to me.'

'Someone special?'

'More than you know.' She lowered her eyelids

so he wouldn't see the tears threatening to pool there. Gabriel was a colleague, nothing more, nothing less. He wasn't interested in her. She would place bets he could have any woman in this room.

He'd ordered more drinks so she lifted her glass towards his. 'What is this? You didn't tell me.'

His eyes flitted from her necklace to her dress—was he looking at her cleavage?—and then back to her drink. 'A strawberry daiquiri.'

'Cheers,' she said, taking a long sip from the straw. 'It's almost as if you guessed what I'd be wearing.' She smiled as she tasted the strawberry daiquiri. 'Red to match my dress, and rum, my favourite flavour. Keep this up and I'll be expecting big things from the night ahead.'

She was holding her breath, hoping he wouldn't realise she'd deflected the conversation. Hoping he'd just accept her answer and move on.

It seemed to take for ever for him to answer. He glanced at his watch. 'The show will start soon. Do you still want to go?'

Her face broke into a beaming smile. 'Absolutely—I've never seen it.'

'Why not? You've been on this boat for months.'

'I'm usually too tired to go and see a show that doesn't start until ten-thirty,' she admitted. 'But tonight I will make an exception, on the proviso, of course, that my boss doesn't give me trouble tomorrow for yawning while on duty!'

They walked along the corridor towards the Whisper Theatre. It was crowded with passengers who had all come to see the popular ten-thirty show. The theatre seated over eight hundred people and, although situated within the ship, its breadth and width covered three internal decks. Francesca and Gabriel filed into the nearest row of seats and sat in the velvet-covered chairs. The lights quickly dimmed and the audience immediately quietened. In the darkened theatre a juggler appeared at the side of the stage, but instead of the usual balls or skittles he was juggling fire-filled torches, which hissed and spat as he threw them in the air. The audience was mesmerised.

Francesca spent the whole time with her brain spinning. She had no idea what was going on. Whatever had shifted between her and Gabriel was terrifying her. She didn't want to be one of the millions blown away by his good looks and TV-star smile.

In the dark theatre, she was also acutely aware of how close she and Gabriel were sitting. Every time their arms brushed against one another she felt a little frisson of excitement tingle up her spine. When she went to change the position of her legs, her crossed leg touched his trouser-clad one and he turned in the darkness and gave her a brief smile. When the show finally finished and the lights came up slowly, Francesca was almost disappointed at being brought back to reality.

'Did you enjoy it?' Gabriel asked.

'It was wonderful.'

They stood back, waiting for the theatre to empty. As the crowd thinned he placed his arm lightly at her back. 'I'll walk you back to your cabin.' He smiled.

'Okay.' Francesca felt her heart dip in disappointment. He hadn't asked her to go back to the bar for another drink. She glanced at her watch. It wasn't that late—was he trying to get rid of her?

The corridor to her cabin was empty. Most people were either already in their cabins or drinking in one of the bars. She stopped outside her door.

'Thanks, Gabriel, that was lovely.' Her eyes were fixed on the floor. She felt awkward and uncomfortable, the ease and relaxation of earlier in the night having left her. Silence hung in the air and neither of them moved.

'So you gave me mouth to mouth?'

Her head shot upwards. Where had that come from? Was he flirting with her? Was he trying to unnerve her?

There was something there. Something hanging in the air between them. Something that kept bringing a smile to her face.

'I did.'

'I'm sorry I can't remember it.' His voice was low, barely loud enough for her to hear. But she did. And it sent a shiver down her spine. 'Shouldn't you have been wearing a red swimsuit for that?'

Her laugh was instantaneous. He'd obviously been having the same thoughts that she'd had. Funny how one TV show had made such a lasting impression.

'In my rush to do the mouth to mouth I forgot

about the red swimsuit,' she quipped. 'But what does it matter? You've already seen it.'

'That I have,' he whispered, stepping forward and closing the gap between them. 'I can't remember if I ever thanked you.'

Then, with the lightest of touches, he bent forward and his hand lightly stroked under her chin. Automatically, she raised her head to meet his. He gave her a slow, sexy smile that sent her pulse racing. His eyes smouldered with fire.

'I can't remember, either,' she whispered. No one else was in the dimly lit corridor. All she could hear was the sound of her heart thudding in her ears. Suddenly he dipped forward and his mouth hovered just millimetres away from hers. She stepped forward as her body reacted unconsciously to his. She felt him hardening against her and as she moved even closer she felt a little groan escape from his lips. She could feel his breath on her cheek, tickling her skin.

Now. Kiss me now.

She closed her eyes. It was inevitable. Any moment now she would feel his lips devouring hers.

Instead his lips brushed against her ear. 'Thank you, Francesca,' he whispered.

He stepped back, his breathing shallow and ragged, his eyes burning.

His breathing slowed. 'Goodnight, *cara.*' His accent stroked across her skin and she watched as his lean, athletic body turned and disappeared down the corridor.

She collapsed back against her door. Wow! Her head was spinning.

She lifted her slightly trembling hand and pushed the cabin card into the slot on her door. The door swung open and she collapsed onto her nearby bed.

He'd almost kissed her but had then walked away. The sparks between them could have set the whole ship alight. She could already imagine the sensations of kissing him. A blow-your-mind, send-you-rocketing-off-into-space, turn-your-legs-to-jelly kind of kiss. She didn't know whether to laugh, cry or chase him along the corridor and drag him back to her room!

Everything was racing through her mind. The man she didn't want to like. The man who had treated her friend so poorly had nearly just kissed her. And she'd let him.

Was she losing her mind?

Gabriel wasn't someone she could ignore. She had to work with him every day. How on earth was she going to deal with this?

Kissing the boss could turn out to be an occupational hazard.

Gabriel stared at his inbox—forty-six emails, all having come in during the last few hours. He glanced at the clock. It was after midnight but he could already tell that sleep was going to elude him tonight. Payroll queries, exporters, poor-quality ink, complaints, late deliveries and a pile of other mundane details. Dealing with the day-to-day enquiries had seemed simple at first but the more he dealt with, the more seemed to come his way. He'd finished one long day and it looked like he'd have an even longer night ahead.

What on earth had he been thinking of? Kissing her. Was he mad?

If she was anything like her friend and money was her motivator then this time tomorrow he could be slapped with a sexual harassment lawsuit.

The thought made his blood run cold.

How well did he really know Francesca?

Not well at all.

Tonight she'd looked beautiful. He'd almost been blown away by how stunning she'd looked in that red dress, with her long hair falling about her shoulders. The few cocktails had certainly relaxed her and made her seem less guarded. Less unapproachable.

But it had been the reaction to his touch that had caught him by surprise. He hadn't been imagining things between them. The slightest brush of skin had electrified them both.

Her stolen glances towards him. The lingering looks between them, lasting just longer than was entirely natural. The way you felt when you couldn't tear your eyes off someone.

And in that darkened corridor, when it had just been the two of them, he'd acted entirely on instinct. And she'd responded, without a doubt.

A single lapse of concentration could result in a huge pile of trouble.

What had he been thinking?

Gabriel banged his hand off the desk. His laptop wobbled, teetering close to the edge of the desk. He pulled it closer, focusing on the unopened emails in front of him.

Work. That's what he would do.
Anything to get his mind off Francesca.
Anything at all.

CHAPTER SEVEN

FRANCESCA stared at the duty roster and felt her stomach plummet. Gabriel had swapped shifts this morning. The sinking feeling of dread continued as her overactive brain sent a million signals all at once.

He'd only swapped a few hours ago. It was obvious he was trying to avoid her. He must be regretting almost kissing her. She cringed. This was a nightmare.

She was beginning to think it hadn't happened. Maybe it was all just a figment of her overactive imagination? So why did it feel like he was body-swerving her?

There was no way they could avoid each other on a cruise ship and with a medical crew as small as they had.

Talk about out of the frying pan and into the fire. They'd gone from one whole heap of tension between them to another entirely.

She hadn't slept a wink last night. No matter how hard she'd tried. Her brain just hadn't let her. She'd eventually got up and tried to compose an email to Jill but nothing had sounded right.

In fact, everything had sounded exactly the way she felt—guilty.

The first email hadn't mentioned Gabriel at all and had been a dead giveaway as complete avoidance.

The second had been too vague.

The third had been too over the top. Nothing had sounded normal. Nothing had sounded like she'd wanted it to. So she'd eventually given up, made herself a cup of coffee and watched the sun rise from the top deck.

She'd worry about the return email to Jill later.

She glanced over the clinic lists. The ship was due to dock in Ephesus, Turkey today and most of the passengers would probably disembark. Any passenger who needed medical attention would try and attend the medical centre early to avoid missing the coach trips ashore. Sure enough, the list for this morning was busy.

David appeared at her shoulder. 'Morning,

Francesca. You okay? You're looking tired. Hope you're not coming down with the same bug as Katherine.'

Francesca shook her head fiercely. 'Just didn't get much sleep last night.'

'You as well?' He raised his eyebrow at her as if she'd just revealed a closely guarded secret.

'What do you mean?'

David shrugged his shoulders. 'Gabriel asked me to swap with him this morning as he didn't sleep last night, either. He said he'd be in around eleven to take over from me.'

'Gabriel didn't sleep, either?' She could barely keep the squeak out of her voice. What did that mean? That he wasn't really avoiding her? That last night had bothered him just as much as it had bothered her? For a second her spirits almost lifted.

David looked up from the chart he was marking. 'Yeah, he was up late into the night, doing some work for his father.'

Her spirits plummeted immediately again. Gabriel hadn't been thinking about her last night at all. She'd probably been the last thing on his mind. He'd been busy doing other things. 'I didn't know he worked for his father,' she said lightly.

David leaned over and put a few ticks on the clinic list. 'Apparently that's why he came back from America. His dad's health isn't too good and Gabriel is taking over some of the day-to-day running of the company. Trying to ease the strain, so to speak.'

'Wouldn't it make more sense for him to stay in Venice?'

David wagged his finger. 'Aha. You'd think so. But apparently if he's too close to home they'll try and drag him into the family business. Strangely enough, they weren't too keen on him becoming a doctor. All right with you if I see these patients? A few of them are follow-ups from the other day and one is a patient in renal failure I'm familiar with.'

'What? Oh, of course.' She nodded absent-mindedly, lifting the list. Gabriel was helping his father? Why hadn't he mentioned it?

They hadn't wanted him to become a doctor? It seemed almost absurd. Most families would be delighted if their son or daughter became a doctor. What an odd reaction.

She cringed. Of course he hadn't mentioned it—she'd hardly rolled out the red carpet for him. He probably thought it was none of her business.

She looked at the first name on her list. The quicker she started, the quicker she could finish. There were a few crew members who'd managed to avoid their medicals for over a month. She could go and track them down. Thoughts around Gabriel's avoidance tactics would have to wait. And they would probably require another cocktail.

She pasted a smile on her face and walked into the waiting room. 'Eleanor Kennedy, please.'

A few hours later she was nearly finished. Just one child to see: a four-year-old who was feeling generally unwell.

Gabriel had swapped places with David half an hour ago but she hadn't set eyes on him as he'd remained locked in the doctor's office with a notorious staff member who was trying to get out of his duties.

'Carly Glencross, please.'

Carly was sitting on her mother's knee, her eyes red, her face flushed and looking generally miserable.

Carly's mother carried her into the treatment room. 'I'm sure it's nothing,' she said, 'probably just a virus, but she's been like this the last few days. She's been really irritable. Can you just check her over?'

'No problem.' Francesca bent down next to Carly. 'Hi, Carly, I'm Fran, the nurse. Is it okay if I take a little look at you?'

Carly eyed her suspiciously before eventually nodding.

Francesca picked up the tympanic thermometer and demonstrated it to Carly. 'I'm just going to put this in your ear to take your temperature. It only takes a second and I press this little button. Okay?'

Carly nodded again. Francesca got the impression she wasn't going to get a word out of her.

She checked her temperature. High. She knelt in front of Carly and checked her face, neck and chest. Her eyes were red and a little sticky— probably some kind of conjunctivitis. She had a blotchy rash over her chest. The lymph glands in her neck were swollen and so were her hands.

'Have you given her something for her fever?'

Mum nodded. 'I'm giving her paracetamol and

ibuprofen alternately. It's not really having much effect and not helping with her other symptoms.'

Francesca made a few notes in the chart. Carly was like a hundred other children she'd seen on the cruise ship or in A and E in her previous role. No specific infection. Just some random virus that spiked a temperature and made the kid miserable for a few days.

'Is she eating anything?'

Mum shook her head. 'I've been feeding her ice lollies to keep her going.'

Francesca nodded. Viruses commonly put kids off their food and it was important to keep them hydrated, particularly when they had a temperature. If ice lollies worked, that was fine.

She was always a little nervous around children. Even though she'd had lots of experience with them in the past, she wasn't specifically trained as a paediatric nurse so she liked to make sure she hadn't missed something.

She walked over to the drawer to pull out a general advice sheet to give to the mother. Her eyes were drawn to Gabriel's door. He normally liked to see all the kids who came to the medical centre. Should she give him a shout?

Carly gave a little cough, so Francesca poured out some water into a cup. 'Do you want to have a little drink?'

Carly nodded, still not speaking, and opened her mouth to take a sip of the water.

Her lips were slightly chapped, with painful cracks at the corners, and her tongue looked slightly swollen.

Francesca took a deep breath. She'd been just about to send this little one away with instructions to come back if there was no improvement in a day or so. But now she wasn't so sure.

Even more than that, she wanted to see how he would react to her. Would he be embarrassed or act as if nothing at all had happened? Her stomach was clenched in a knot. It was better to get this over and done with.

'If you don't mind, I'm going to get our doctor to take a quick look at Carly. He's a paediatrician, so it's probably best if he sees her, too.'

Just at that Gabriel's door opened. The crew member stormed off and Gabriel's face was like thunder. They'd obviously had words.

It was a shock seeing him after last night. For the first time she noticed every inch of his face—the tiny lines around his eyes, the furrows on his brow and the tense expression when he caught sight of her. It was just as she'd expected. He was dreading the thought of seeing her after last night. He probably had a million lines prepared to try and fob her off. As if she'd give him the chance.

'Dr Russo,' she said briskly, 'could you have a look at Carly Glencross, please?'

Gabriel seemed to snap to attention. He crossed the room in a few steps, the automatic smile appearing on his face at the sight of the little girl and her mother. If only he'd smiled like that for her.

'What have you got?'

Francesca handed over the chart with the notes she'd made. 'Carly's four and has been sick for the last few days. She has a temperature, conjunctivitis and a blotchy rash. The lymph glands are up in her neck. Mum just wondered if there was anything else we could do for her.'

Gabriel knelt down and spoke in a soft voice to Carly. 'Well, hello there, princess.'

Gabriel only took a few minutes to examine

Carly carefully, listening to her heart and lungs, looking in her throat and examining her hands.

He ran his fingers across the palms of her hands. They were slightly oedematous with the skin particularly red on the palms and peeling slightly around her nails.

'What are you looking for?' Francesca felt uneasy. What did Gabriel suspect? Some of Carly's symptoms were a little out of the ordinary and for some reason they were now setting off alarm bells in her head.

He'd barely made eye contact with her since he'd left his room. Was this how it was going to be between them now? Avoidance and aloofness?

'Stick your tongue out for me, please, Carly.'

She did, with pleasure, pulling a face at Gabriel.

'Strawberry-coloured tongue. Get me some aspirin please, Francesca.'

'But kids can't have aspirin, Gabriel, it's dangerous for under twelves.' Her words were automatic. Surely, as a paediatrician, he should know that?

Francesca may not have been trained as a

paediatric nurse and normally she coped well but right now she was feeling out of her depth. But there were some golden rules that had been drummed into her by the sister of the A and E department where she'd previously worked. Aspirin being dangerous for under twelves was one of them.

He shook his head. 'In these circumstances it's exactly what we need.'

Gabriel stood up and made a few notes. He touched the side of Carly's face and gave her a little smile. 'You have been the best patient I've seen today. Would you like a fairy sticker?'

He pulled some from a roll attached to the wall. 'You pick the one you like best.'

Carly bent over the roll of fairy stickers, examining their colourful dresses. The stickers were used widely for the kids that attended the medical centre—fairies for girls and dinosaurs for boys.

'Could you bring over the ECG machine, please, Francesca?'

An ECG for a kid? Did a child's ECG look different from an adult's? Francesca didn't even know.

Cardiac. He thought it was a cardiac condition. She had a mad flash.

He sat down next to Carly's mum. 'Have you heard of Kawasaki disease?'

The woman almost did a double-take at the strange-sounding disorder. Her face automatically paled and she shook her head. 'No. What on earth is that? Is that what's wrong with Carly?'

Gabriel nodded. 'It's not widely known. It's a kind of autoimmune disorder that causes inflammation, particularly around the blood vessels.' He touched Carly's palms. 'It has a whole set of classic symptoms. The red palms and peeling skin is one of them, as is the strawberry-coloured tongue, persistent temperature and cracked lips.'

Francesca had wheeled the ECG machine over and felt frozen at the bottom of the bed. Kawasaki disease? Oh, no.

She'd just remembered. A kid from one of her days in A and E. Just like this.

A kid where the key indicator had been peeling skin on the soles of his feet.

She automatically walked over to Carly and

removed her socks. Sure enough, peeling skin on the soles of her feet.

She held one foot aloft.

'Gabriel?'

He nodded.

She should have caught this. Yes, it was unusual but she'd come across this before.

The sinking feeling in her stomach wasn't going to go away.

She'd done it again. The one thing she'd said she'd never do.

She'd been distracted by Gabriel.

And she'd missed something. She'd missed *this*. Her head had been too full of Gabriel and the night before to concentrate on the patient in front of her.

Distracted by the playboy doc.

It made her feel physically sick. The fallout from the last time had affected her father. The time it could have been a kid.

Gabriel swung Carly's legs up on to the bed and laid her back against the pillows. 'I'm just going to get a little tracing of your heart, Carly.' He held up the leads from the ECG machine. 'I just need to attach these onto your chest.'

It only took him a few seconds and Francesca pressed the buttons. The heart tracing spat out the other side of the machine a few moments later.

'What does this mean for Carly?' Mrs Glencross's voice was becoming higher.

'First, we give her some aspirin. That's the first line of treatment for Kawasaki disease. Carly should really have some bloods taken and a chest X-ray, too. I'm going to phone the local paediatric unit here and talk to their consultant. It might be better for her to have the rest of her tests done there.'

'We need to leave the ship?'

Gabriel nodded. 'Carly will need to be admitted to hospital. Kawasaki disease can cause complications in children.'

'What kind of complications?'

Francesca could see him bite his bottom lip, as if trying to decide how much information to give. 'Some kids can develop inflammation around the blood vessels at the heart. They need to be monitored closely. Carly will need to have a scan of her heart. There's also another drug treatment called gammoglobulin that can be given. But it's a treatment that needs to be administered in hospital.'

Carly's mother sagged back against the wall. 'I thought she just had a bit of a cold, or a virus. I'd no idea it could be anything like this.'

Gabriel reached over and took her hand. 'I'm going to give Carly some aspirin in the meantime. Let me make a call to the local hospital and then I'll tell you what happens next.'

Francesca rechecked Carly's observations and gave her the aspirin that Gabriel had prescribed.

She tried to make herself busy, making tea for Mrs Glencross and phoning her husband to come and join them in the medical unit. They had docked at Ephesus that morning with Kusadasi being the nearest large town. Francesca knew it had two large, well-equipped hospitals—one public and one private—but she had no idea about the paediatric facilities.

She walked into Gabriel's office just as he was replacing the phone.

'What kind of complications can Kawasaki disease cause?' She tried to keep the tremble from her voice. It had been obvious to her that he'd been trying to stick to the basics for Carly's shocked mother. She couldn't remember what had happened to her last patient.

That was the trouble with A and E, the patients came through so quickly with little or no chance of follow-up.

He leaned back in his chair. 'The ambulance will be here in half an hour to transport Carly to the paediatric unit.' His heavy eyelids lifted, meeting her gaze for the first time that day. He watched her for a few seconds before answering. 'The inflammation of the blood vessels can affect the coronary arteries. One in five kids with Kawasaki disease will develop inflammation of the coronary arteries. It can lead to an aneurysm.'

He picked a pencil from his desk, twiddling it through his fingers as if concentrating deeply. 'That's why we give aspirin—to try and reduce the inflammation. Even kids who have been treated can still develop an aneurysm. This is serious stuff. One per cent of kids with this disease die. And it can have lasting impacts. Carly will need to be monitored for the rest of her life.'

An aneurysm. Francesca's head spun around to the treatment room where Carly was sitting with her mum and newly arrived dad. That little girl could have a life-threatening condition. And she'd almost sent her back to her cabin with a basic child-with-a-viral-infection sheet.

She could have sentenced that child to death. All because she'd almost missed something essential.

Her legs felt like jelly underneath her.

'Francesca, are you okay? You're very pale.' Gabriel was standing next to her, his hand touching her shoulder.

She couldn't look at him. She couldn't look him in the eye.

After her earlier thoughts about him avoiding eye contact with her, the irony was that now *she* couldn't look at him.

If she did, he would see it. He would be able to read her like a book. He'd know the mistake she'd almost made.

She couldn't bear to look at him. She couldn't bear to think she might have based her decision to get Carly a second opinion on the fact she'd wanted to see Gabriel.

It made her feel pathetic. And absolutely useless at her job.

What if she'd sent that child back to her cabin? What if she'd developed an aneurysm that had ruptured at sea?

She'd been so close to doing that. So very close…

'Francesca.' His voice was firm and he had a hand on either shoulder, standing in front of her and looking her square in the eye.

'Can you phone a ship's porter to help the family with their packing and luggage? We don't have a lot of time here.'

She nodded numbly. It was time to go on autopilot. She could do this. She could get through this.

Gabriel was still talking. 'The hospital is going to carry out her blood tests and chest X-ray. We just need to write a transfer.' He glanced over his shoulder. 'And I need to have another word with the parents.'

Francesca nodded again. Phone the porter, instruct him to pack up the cabin. She could do that.

She turned towards the office, ready to make the phone call.

'Good call, Francesca.'

The words stopped her in her tracks. 'What?' It was the last thing she'd expected.

Gabriel was giving her a knowing smile. 'It was a good pick-up. Lots of people would have missed that. You didn't.' He turned and walked back into the treatment room.

Francesca held her breath. He had no idea. No idea at all.

But I almost did miss it.

Her heart was pounding in her chest. It was making her head swim and sending tingles down her arms—and not in a good way.

This could have held a very different outcome for that little girl. An outcome based on *her* poor instincts. It didn't matter how hard she tried to work at it. Her worst fear had been realised.

She really had lost her nursing instincts. They were dead. Gone.

Or maybe they weren't. Maybe it was all about distraction.

She'd allowed herself to get distracted by Gabriel instead of focusing on the job.

How could she admit the truth to anyone? That the reason she'd asked for a second opinion hadn't been based on the little girl's condition but her own selfish, misplaced desires. What kind of a person did that make her?

Everything about this had been a bad idea. From the second she'd set eyes on Gabriel she'd known he was going to be trouble. As for last night? That had been a joke. Something to push out of her mind and forget about.

She had to concentrate on her work. Concentrate on her duties as a nurse. This couldn't be about her. This had to about her patients.

She picked up the phone and dialled the porter automatically. She grabbed Carly's chart and transferred the written remarks into the electronic record, ready for Gabriel to print out for the transfer.

The porter was going to meet them portside with the family's luggage. There would be no room for it in the ambulance, so it would have to be transported in a taxi. Francesca made another quick call to the cruise company representatives to organise someone to meet the family locally and sort out accommodation for them.

There. That was everything she could do right now. So why were her hands still trembling?

She'd seen this condition with its unusual set

of symptoms before. She should have picked it up. And she would have—if she hadn't been so distracted by Gabriel.

She stood up and walked back through to the treatment room. Gabriel had just lifted Carly and seated her in a wheelchair.

There was no getting away from it, the little girl and her family looked frightened. Gabriel was doing his best to put them at ease: he'd managed to find a book for Carly to read and was telling her about his favourite character as he tucked a blanket around her knees.

She still looked unwell, but no more unwell than dozens of other children Francesca had seen in her life as a nurse. How many other kids could she have sent home with this condition?

The thought sent a shiver down her spine and the hairs at the back of her neck tingling.

The phone next to her rang. 'Ambulance is here, Gabriel,' she said as she replaced the receiver. 'I've also spoken to the main office. Marie, a company rep, will meet Mr and Mrs Glencross at the hospital and sort out accommodation for them. The family luggage will be transferred by taxi.'

Gabriel gave her a nod. 'That's great, Francesca, I'd been so busy organising things with the hospital I hadn't considered that.'

He grabbed the handles of the wheelchair and turned to the parents. 'I'll walk you down to the ambulance. You can man the medical centre, can't you, Francesca?'

She nodded and he pushed the chair out the door. His voice drifted along the corridor, 'Dr Demir will be waiting for you, he's fully informed about Carly's condition and will be able to carry out the rest of her tests...'

Francesca sagged against the wall of the treatment room. The rest of the medical centre was empty and it was just as well as she didn't think she could cope with seeing anyone right now.

Tears pooled at the corners of her eyes. She sat down in front of the computer and opened one of the search engines. Kawasaki disease. A mediocre collection of symptoms that she could so easily have missed.

The temperature, rash, joint pains and sore throat and tongue could be attributed to just about any childhood ailment. Irritability, sore eyes, swollen lymph glands, going off food all seemed so run of the mill to her.

But the key indicators of the disease—the strawberry-coloured tongue, red palms and soles of feet and the peeling skin on hands or feet—were often used to help the diagnosis.

She'd missed them.

If she hadn't ever heard of this disease before, she could forgive herself.

But she *had* seen it before. And she couldn't forgive herself for missing it.

A handsome doctor was no excuse.

But Gabriel hadn't. He hadn't missed anything.

Her brain was ticking furiously. Would Katherine have made the same assumption? Would Kevin? Would David Marsh have picked it up? Or was it only the fact that Gabriel was a paediatrician that had gone in Carly's favour?

She couldn't even bear to think about it.

The tears started to trickle down her face.

Gabriel had praised her. He'd looked her straight in the eye and told her she'd done a good job.

But he'd had no idea she'd just wanted to see him. To see what his reaction to her would be.

He'd had no idea she had been wondering if he was as confused about the night before as she was.

She pulled herself up straight.

There was no way she could let this happen again.

She had to forget about Gabriel and just focus on her job.

She couldn't allow the slightest distraction— no matter how handsome.

CHAPTER EIGHT

GABRIEL was relieved to wave the Glencross family off. Dr Demir at the local hospital had sounded confident he could deal with the condition. Carly would be in safe hands.

That was the second time Francesca had surprised him. The second time her instincts had been spot on.

Why was she so unsure of herself? She'd looked like a startled rabbit when he'd told her she'd made a good call.

But maybe that wasn't about her clinical abilities. Maybe it was about him.

In a sense he was relieved. He'd picked up something in a child that others might have missed—something that could have had devastating consequences.

Every time it happened he felt his stomach clench in endless knots at the thought of a child suffering—of something being missed. He was determined it would never happen on his watch.

He'd been there. He'd seen the effect on a family that losing a child could have. He'd experienced it firsthand.

His brother had only been a baby, not even a year old, when he'd died. And Gabriel had never forgotten his mother. She'd known something was wrong. Even when the local doctor had tried to fob her off and tell her Dante would be fine in a few days.

More than anything Gabriel remembered the scream. Dante's high-pitched scream—the scream of a baby with meningitis—had imprinted on him for life.

Once heard, never forgotten.

But by then it had been too late. A hasty trip to the hospital in the dead of night had resulted in some emergency treatment but it had all been in vain.

The day they had buried the little white coffin in the ground at the Isola di San Michele—Venice's cemetery—had haunted him.

For a six-year-old boy it had been hard to understand the impact on the family. He'd only known that nothing would ever be the same again. Over the years his mother had never lost the sadness in her eyes and his father had flung himself into the family business, as if immersing himself would dull the pain.

It hadn't helped that their family's loss had been widely reported in the media by nosy and intrusive reporters.

Dante had been their 'little blessing', their *piccola benedizione*. His mother had thought she couldn't have any more children after the birth of his younger sister, so the arrival of Dante had been greeted with much celebration.

And for years after Dante's death Gabriel and his sister had been afraid to mention his name. They'd kept a photograph of him in a locked cabinet in their room, taking it out and staring at the little smiling face on occasion.

He'd lost most of his childhood after that. His father had barely been in the house—only eating and sleeping there.

It had been obvious his father loved them but the house had held too many painful memories for him. So he'd spent more and more time at work. Long hours, stress and ignoring his physical health over the years had taken its toll. It was no wonder he was a victim of heart disease—the disease that was slowly killing him.

Even as a child Gabriel had felt all the responsibility for his mother. Was it survivor's guilt? Trying to stick the family back together? Trying to distract her in any way possible to lessen the pain behind her eyes?

The only time he'd ever felt like a child again had been during the long summers they'd spent with his father's cousin and his family in Pisa. It had been the only time he'd ever felt relieved of the burden of family.

And for Gabriel every time a child came before him like this, every time a child with a vague set of symptoms appeared, he reminded himself why he did this job. No child should suffer the way Dante had. And no family should suffer the way they had.

Twenty-five years was a long time, but time didn't lessen the pain. Sometimes it only enhanced it. Only those who truly didn't understand thought that time could be a healer. Those who had suffered a similar loss knew the truth.

One of Gabriel's colleagues had lost a child

some years before, and he was the only person Gabriel had ever confided in, sharing his pain as only a fellow sufferer could.

Frank had told him that every year was harder than the one before, particularly as the milestones of life approached. Time to start school, time to leave school, time to have girlfriends, special birthdays, time to make career choices— all things that his son and Gabriel's brother had missed out on.

And Gabriel had noticed little marks on the calendar that his mother kept. It had taken him a few years to work out what they were. Dante's birthday. The day of Dante's death. A star had marked the day he would have been eighteen. A little red triangle the day he would have graduated from school.

Gone but never forgotten.

Families. So much joy, but so much pain. That was why he never objected to the reputation the media had labelled him with. Millionaire playboy. Playboy doc. In a way it was easier for him. Women had fewer expectations of him. None of them were expecting a wedding band and a house with a white picket fence.

He'd made sure of that.

And spent most of his time focused on his work. A job that he usually relished.

But no matter how hard he tried to be relaxed in his role, there were always times it took him back to his childhood. And that's when it was essential for him to be in control.

That's when he got ratty. For some people being a doctor was just a job. But for Gabriel this was a chance for salvation. He might not have been able to save his brother but so far his decisions had probably saved the lives of over a hundred other children. A hundred children who had got to live another day with their families, to run around in the summer sunshine and enjoy a carefree existence instead of being buried in the cold, damp earth.

Precious, precious lives.

He was in charge now. Not some hopeless doctor who'd been more interested in getting back to his bed than caring for Gabriel's sick brother.

He always took the time with patients and their families. He always went that extra mile. No one should suffer the same fate as the Russo family. No one at all.

His phone buzzed in his pocket and he pulled it out to check the message. His father. Again.

Gabriel sighed. No rest for the wicked.

Katherine had folded her arms across her chest. 'So spill.' She looked serious and she didn't normally take no for an answer.

Francesca tried her best to look innocent as she restocked one of the cupboards. The last thing she wanted to do was talk about Gabriel.

'I don't know what you're talking about.'

'Yes, you do, lady. I heard after the dinner the other night you and Dr Delicious went for drinks. What happened?'

What happened? It was a good question and one that she'd no idea how to answer.

'How did you end up going for drinks with him anyway? I thought you hated him?'

'I do. I mean…I did.'

'Aha.' Katherine slid along the counter towards her. 'Now that definitely sounds interesting.'

Francesca felt cornered. What was she going to say anyway? I spent all night trying to decide if I liked him or not and then he gave me the most earth-shattering whisper of a kiss and walked away?

She'd had butterflies in her stomach when he'd kissed her. She'd been too excited—like a pathetic teenager—to think any further ahead.

But the morning after she'd woken up with a terrible feeling in the pit of her stomach. *He'd walked away.*

What did that say about her? He wasn't interested? She wasn't interesting enough? She wasn't sexy enough?

The fact was she'd no idea why he'd walked away or what he was thinking.

Was he planning on doing it again? Or was she just going to have to spend the next few weeks working around him, wondering if anything would happen? Because that wasn't her style. Not at all.

And she'd no intention of being a shrinking violet, hanging around waiting to see if she could get a part of him.

Sure, he was handsome. Sure, he was sexy. Sure, for a few milliseconds she'd actually considered pulling him into her cabin and doing the midnight tango with him.

But he was also her boss.

And she had to work with him every day.

And most days she liked work. Or she used to. Her colleagues were a good team, they were a fun team and she didn't want to do anything to spoil that.

Besides, she was waiting for her visa for Australia, and surely—*surely*—it must be arriving any day now. She'd been repeating this mantra for the last six weeks. The last thing she needed was to have some mad fling with some Italian dreamboat.

Flings weren't her style. Flirting? Well, maybe. That she could control. Then she could decide when to back off and when to proceed.

Maybe things had just gone a little too far?

But she could sort that. She could talk to him. It would be fine.

So why was she talking to herself in her head?

Her eyes met Katherine's. The interrogator hadn't moved and Francesca felt her cheeks start to flush again.

'Nothing happened.'

Katherine raised her perfectly plucked eyebrows. 'Oh, really?' Her voice dripped with good-humoured sarcasm. 'And the band played "Believe it if you like".'

'No. Really, it didn't. We went to watch the show together, had a drink and that was it.'

Katherine nodded her head towards the computer. 'So, in that case, you wouldn't be interested in anything I'd found online about our resident dreamy Italian?'

Francesca hesitated, just a fraction of a second. She could resist the temptation, couldn't she? She could feign disinterest convincingly.

Nope. She couldn't. Rats.

'What is it?' She crossed the tiny dispensing room in one second flat and sat down at the computer screen.

A gorgeous image of Gabriel in a tux glared back at her. Wow. This photo could rival the Mediterranean white-trunked Adonis that had adorned Jill's bedside cabinet.

But in this one he didn't look happy. And, wow—what about the woman surgically attached to his arm? Hanging on there like some piranha?

Beautiful, blonde, in an emerald-green to-die-for figure-hugging dress. The kind of woman who had the proportions of a Barbie doll, proportions no woman was supposed to obtain naturally. The woman was beautiful, perfectly formed, with exquisite features and wearing a dress that must have cost more than Francesca earned in a month.

Only problem was the ice-cold look on her face.

That face could have sunk the *Titanic*.

'Where on earth is this from?'

Katherine looked smug. 'Oh, so now you're interested, are you?' Her head shot down next to Francesca's, just inches away from her face. 'I thought nothing happened?'

Francesca stared her out, trying her absolute best to keep her face free from anything that might give away the stomach that was currently churning, probably giving her an ulcer as they spoke.

She shrugged her shoulders. 'Let's just say I'm as curious as the rest of the crew about our doctor.'

She read the caption under the photo: *'Heir to the Russo printing fortune, Gabriel Russo, with Felice Audair at the annual Venetian charity ball.'*

Katherine peered at the screen a little longer. 'Last year's charity ball. I don't think you need to worry,' she said assuredly. 'Look at their faces and their body language.'

'Do I have to?' Francesca's voice was becoming higher pitched by the second.

'Yes,' said Katherine determinedly, 'you do.' She pointed at the screen. 'He might have his arm around her but look at his face, there's no affection there.' She glanced at Francesca. 'And look at her eyes, they're like glass—she isn't really interested in him.' She paused a few seconds then added, 'You've nothing to worry about.'

'Who said I was worried?' Her self-defence mechanism had kicked in.

Francesca's eyes hadn't left the screen. 'Do you think that could be a relative?' she asked half-heartedly, knowing the answer even before she heard the reply. Katherine snorted. 'Not a chance—with those calculating looks I would be more likely to call her a predator than anything else.' She shrugged. 'At least the name matches the looks. She sounds like a prime-time TV villain.'

Francesca sagged back into the chair. She

clicked on the links away from the photographs, her eyes scanning the page that came up before her.

It seemed as if at one point Gabriel had been photographed wherever he went. It must have driven him nuts. He seemed permanently surrounded by a bevy of beauties. What did it feel like to have your life examined under a microscope?

She'd no idea how famous he was in Italy. It appeared he couldn't move without someone reporting it. It seemed almost obvious to her why he'd left.

So why come back?

And just how ill was his father?

Then there were all the listings for paediatric journal articles all with his name attached. Published papers. He was obviously dedicated to his job.

And a whole host of other, older headlines—mainly in Italian. Something about a tragedy. But she didn't have time to read because Katherine had clicked on another link.

She wrinkled her nose. 'I don't get it. He's a millionaire, with a whole host of specialist skills.'

She turned to face Francesca. 'I mean, I'm glad that he's here but what *is* he doing here?'

Francesca felt herself bristle. David had mentioned his father being sick but maybe no one else knew. Maybe it was a secret. 'He must have his reasons.'

Katherine had her hand at her mouth. 'I wonder what they are.' She turned to face Francesca. 'Did you find out anything? You're the one who's been for drinks with him.'

Francesca shook her head. 'I was only there as a human shield. Guarding him from the circling bunch of cougars in the Atlantic Bar. He said I owed him after the week before.'

The answer seemed to placate Katherine. She shrugged. 'Yeah, you probably did. Did that family get away okay?'

'What family?'

'The kid, with the Kawa…whatever-it's-called disease, the potential heart condition.'

A chill crept down Francesca's spine. Of course Katherine would have heard about that. The medical unit was small so any unusual cases were always discussed.

'Yeah. She was admitted to the paediatric unit

in the hospital in Kusadasi.' She hesitated, wondering for a second if she should actually say the words. What would Katherine think?

'Did you have a look at the notes?'

Katherine was carrying a pile of boxes of rubber gloves ready to stock in the cupboard. 'Not yet. David said he would look over them later with me—just because it was such an unusual case.'

Francesca took a deep breath. 'Do you think you would have picked up on it?'

Katherine looked surprised. 'The Kawa-whatsit disease? Not a chance.' She shook her head. 'David wasn't sure he would have either. That's why we were going to discuss it later.'

'I almost missed it.' The words were out before she could stop them and the expression on her face must have said it all, because Katherine sat back down opposite her and put her hand on her shoulder.

'But you didn't.'

'But I've seen it before. I should have remembered. The symptoms are so remarkable—the strawberry tongue, cracked lips, peeling skin.'

Katherine stayed silent for a minute. 'How long since you've seen it?'

Francesca trawled her brain. 'A couple of years, in an A and E in Southampton.'

Katherine nodded, obviously choosing her words carefully. 'The symptoms are unusual and I hope I'll remember them. But I can't guarantee it. You've seen hundreds of patients since then. And everything's fine. You asked for a second opinion, that's what matters.' She squeezed Francesca's shoulder. 'And you won't miss it again.'

Francesca bit her tongue. She'd said enough. It wouldn't do to tell her colleague the rest. That the real reason she'd missed it had been because her mind had been on a man. She couldn't let that happen again.

Francesca tried to appear calm. She gave a little smile and pushed herself up from the chair, away from the computer screen. 'I'm going to go and chase up some of the crew who have missed their medicals. They keep avoiding us, so I'm getting suspicious.'

Katherine nodded. 'Let's go up for a coffee first then I'll give you a hand. One of the engineers has steadily avoided us for over a month.'

She gave Francesca a wink. 'I think it might be two-girl job.'

Ten minutes later they had just sat down to a well-deserved cappuccino in the Clipper Lounge when the piercing shrill of Francesca's emergency page sounded. *'Emergency Deck Five, Drake's Dining Room'.*

'Blooming typical.' Francesca sprang from her seat, leaving her steaming coffee untouched.

'Want help?' Katherine yelled after her.

'No, it's fine,' Francesca shouted over her shoulder. 'David or Gabriel will have the other on-call page. One of them will appear.'

She ran to the nearest stairwell and grabbed the emergency bag, which was stowed in a discreet hatch. Deck five was two decks beneath her and the dining room was immediately adjacent to the stairwell. She glanced at her watch as she reached the dining-room doors—ten to six, almost time for the first sitting. The dining room wasn't open yet to the passengers, which meant the incident had to involve a member of the crew. An anxious waiter was waiting to meet her at the doors. 'This way,' he said worriedly. 'I think he's having a seizure.'

Francesca hurried over to where the crewman was lying on the floor, surrounded by a throng of worried colleagues. She pushed the onlookers out of her way. 'Let me through, please,' she ordered, her voice loud and commanding. They obediently stepped to one side to let her pass and she knelt on the floor next to the patient. Someone had had the good sense to attempt to put him in the recovery position, so he was lying on his side, but was still jerking and twitching, with his colleague's hands trying to steady him.

'Does anyone know what happened?' she asked the sea of surrounding faces. She bent her head over the patient and her heart lurched—it was Roberto Franc.

As soon as she'd identified him, it was obvious what was wrong.

But like any good nurse Francesca started with the obvious—airway, breathing and circulation. His airway was unobstructed and clear. He was definitely breathing, his chest rising and falling rapidly. Her fingers felt the pulse in his wrist, holding it firmly as his limbs continued to twitch intermittently.

'He was disorientated and muttering,' one

of the fellow busboys started. 'I kept asking him what was wrong but his eyes were really glazed, it was if he couldn't hear me. Then he just dropped to the floor and started twitching'.

Francesca quickly checked him over. She wouldn't be able to get him to eat or drink anything as his consciousness level was too altered and he would risk choking. He didn't appear to have injured himself in the fall so she pulled the blood-testing meter out of the emergency bag and quickly tested his blood-sugar level. The meter only took five seconds to produce a result. One point four mmol/litre. His reading was way below normal. Francesca knew the average person had a blood glucose ranging between four and seven mmol/litre.

Roberto's blood glucose was so low it had caused him to lose consciousness.

A few seconds later Gabriel appeared at her side. He was obviously out of breath and she could feel the heat emanating from his body as he crouched beside her.

'Where on earth were you?' The medical centre was only one deck below; there was no way he could be so out of breath running up one flight of stairs.

He smiled and shrugged, 'The sports deck.'

'Deck Sixteen? Why didn't you use the lift?'

He gave a fake shudder. 'Too slow. Stops at every floor.' His eyes swept over their patient. 'Isn't this the young man you saw recently?'

She nodded and lifted the glucometer to show him the reading.

'Got any glucagon?'

She opened her nearby emergency bag and pulled out a bright orange box, flipping it open. The glucagon hydrochloride injection was only used in extreme circumstances and would help deliver glucose quickly to the body and bring Roberto out of his hypoglycaemic coma. The same injection was commonly carried by ambulances and used in accident and emergency departments.

'Want me to do that?'

Gabriel found a suitable bit of skin and administered the injection swiftly and waited for it to take effect.

'He's diabetic,' he said to the watching crowd. 'His blood sugar has dropped to a dangerously low level. This injection will bring him round but it takes a few minutes to work.'

'Diabetic? But he looked as if he was having a seizure,' said one of the confused waiters.

Francesca gave a rueful smile. 'It can look like that. When a diabetic's blood sugar drops, the symptoms can vary from person to person. Some people shake, sweat and become confused, eventually all will lose consciousness, and sometimes their bodies can twitch or shake a little— it doesn't happen to everyone.'

She gave another quick look at Roberto. 'See? His twitching is starting to reduce as the glucose is beginning to take effect.'

'You must have done this a few times,' Gabriel murmured.

Francesca felt herself stiffen. She didn't want to talk about her dad. Her self-defence mechanism went onto autopilot. 'My dad was usually well controlled. He only ever needed glucogon a few times in his life.'

Gabriel looked puzzled for a second, then his face softened and he reached over and touched her hand, his warm skin encompassing hers.

'I wasn't talking about your dad, Fran. I was talking about being a nurse in general.'

Francesca held her breath. Of course. His brown eyes were fixed on hers, a barrage of questions stored in them. She swallowed and looked away quickly. She had a patient to treat and looked up at the staff around them. 'He was supposed to be allowed to take a break to eat before service started. Does anyone know what happened?'

A couple of the busboys shot each other uneasy looks.

Francesca shook her head impatiently. She didn't have time for this. 'Okay, tell me now what happened.'

'Well,' started one reluctantly, 'he asked earlier if he could stop for something, but the dining-room manager wouldn't let him.'

Francesca's face became thunderous. 'What?'

'Get back to work!' The dining-room manager stormed up behind the crowd of onlookers, having obviously heard the preceding remark. Before the spectators could disperse, another voice cut through the air.

Gabriel was on his feet, his face furious. 'You

and I are going to have words, sir.' His voice was louder, commanding, dripping with ice. He cut a path through the crowd of bystanders. He stopped directly in front of the manager. 'Your actions…' he squinted at the badge on his jacket '…Enzo, would make you directly responsible for this young man's condition.'

He pointed to Roberto, who now lay still on the floor. 'It would also make you directly answerable to me,' he continued sternly. 'I know that the medical centre had left strict instructions regarding Mr Franc's condition and the fact he needed extra breaks to allow him to eat.'

Gabriel was now directly face to face with Enzo, his arms folded firmly across his chest. There was no way he was going to allow his authority to be questioned. Enzo's face had turned a beetroot shade of red. 'We were too busy,' he spat. 'I have two members of staff off sick and I can't afford to babysit anybody!'

'When I give advice I expect it to be followed.' Gabriel's voice was low, menacing—the voice of a man getting ready to lose his temper.

Enzo waved his hand dismissively. 'I have a dining room to open and passengers waiting outside to be fed—when will you be ready to move him?' He turned his nose up disparagingly at Roberto.

Francesca could see the rage flaring in Gabriel's eyes. He stepped forward, his nose practically touching the other man's. 'You can open your dining room when *I* say so and not a second before that,' he hissed.

Francesca tugged at his trouser leg, anything to try and diffuse the conflict. 'Dr Russo, can you give me a hand, please?'

Her words appeared to jolt Gabriel from his concentrated fury. He knelt down next to her. 'How is he?'

'He's going to be fine—but I'm not so sure I can say the same for you.' She was worried about him—he had looked as if he'd been about to erupt. 'I thought it best to distract you before you landed a punch on him.'

'I almost did. Stupid man. Medical orders stand, no matter what else is going on in the ship. He had no right to refuse Roberto time to eat. I'll be taking this up with the captain.'

His anger seemed to dissipate while he was talking to Francesca. She rested her hand on his forearm. 'Now you've calmed down a little, do you think you could give Kevin a call and ask him to bring a wheelchair up? Roberto's starting to come round now and I'd like to get him down to the medical centre.'

Gabriel leaned over Roberto, whose eyes had flickered open. 'What happened?' he groaned, clutching his forehead. He tried to sit up but couldn't quite get his balance. Gabriel put his arm around Roberto's shoulders and helped him straighten up.

'It's all right, Roberto. You had a hypoglycaemic attack. We had to give you a glucose injection to bring you round.'

'Oh, no.' He groaned, leaning forward and putting his head in his hand.

'I'm just going to arrange a wheelchair for you and we'll take you down to the medical centre for a few hours.' He gave Francesca a brief glance before striding off to the nearest phone.

Francesca caught the arm of the nearest waiter. 'Can you go to the kitchen and get me some sandwiches for Roberto, please?' The waiter gave a quick nod and dashed off.

'How are you feeling, Roberto?'

'Sick. I feel really sick.'

'Unfortunately that's one of the side-effects of the injection we gave you. It can make some people feel nauseous. Once I've got you downstairs I'll start by giving you a cup of tea and see how you feel from there. The injection gives you a boost of glucose, but it would be better if I could get you to eat something.'

Now that Roberto had regained consciousness, some of the dining-room staff had started to disperse to prepare for the influx of passengers. Francesca could hear the voices of the passengers outside the main doors. They were obviously confused about why the dining room hadn't opened yet. A few seconds later she could hear Kevin's voice as he attempted to make his way through the throng. 'Excuse me, folks, can you let me through? We've got a bit of an emergency in the dining room—the sooner you let me through, the sooner I can deal with it.'

Seconds later he emerged red-faced through the dining room doors, pushing a wheelchair. 'Phew!' he said. 'That did the trick. For a minute there I thought they weren't going to move for me.' He parked the wheelchair next to Francesca and Roberto. 'Can I give you a hand?'

Together they helped a still shaky and slightly disorientated Roberto into the chair. 'Where's Gabriel?' asked Kevin as he started to push the wheelchair in the direction of the main doors.

Francesca indicated her head to the side. 'He's on the phone. I take it he's filling the captain in on his displeasure.' She caught hold of the nearest door and swung it open, balancing the plate of sandwiches for Roberto in the other. They were met by an array of anxious faces. 'Excuse me, please,' she said briskly, 'If you would let us past, I'm sure the dining room will be able to open in a few minutes.'

The crowd parted and they made their way over to the nearest lift. In a matter of minutes they were back at the medical centre.

Kevin and Francesca helped Roberto onto one of the nearest beds. 'I'll just start a chart,' said Francesca, lifting one down from above the bed.

'I'll check his blood-glucose level again,' said Kevin. 'What was it originally?'

'One point four.'

Kevin rolled his eyes. 'No wonder he hit the deck.'

The alarm sounded as Kevin checked the blood level. 'Well, it's up a bit. Three point nine. The injection must have started working.'

Roberto was pale and looked exhausted. Having a hypoglycaemic attack of this level often made patients feel very tired. Francesca knew that Roberto would be best if he was allowed to sleep for a while. She finished writing up his chart. 'I'm just going to get you a cup of tea.' She smiled at him. 'I know you're tired. I'll let you go to sleep once you've had something to eat. We'll keep an eye on your blood-glucose levels over the next few hours. Don't worry if you feel us stabbing your finger while you're sleeping.'

Kevin came and joined her in the nearby consulting room where the kettle was stored. 'Do you want me to do that? I don't mind, I'm due to be on duty anyway.'

'It's okay, Kevin, I don't mind waiting a bit longer. I've got some other patients that I should probably update you on before evening surgery.'

'By the way, there's mail for you.'

He pointed to an official-looking envelope with a tell-tale insignia on one of the worktops.

She drew a sharp breath. Her Australian visa—it had finally arrived. She stuffed the envelope into her pocket. 'Have you mentioned this to anyone?'

He shook his head and shrugged his shoulders. 'Your business, Francesca. No one else's.'

She gave him a smile. 'Thanks, Kevin.'

He gave her a nod and headed back out to Roberto. She finished making the tea and picked up the plate of sandwiches. She knew he was feeling sick but she would have to try and entice him to eat something before he went to sleep.

'Whoa!'

Gabriel let out the cry as Francesca walked out the door and almost crashed straight into him. He caught her hand to stop her spilling the tea.

'I see you're in a better mood. Did you manage to speak to the captain?'

'That's where I've just came from. All medical orders on this ship stand. Enzo will be spoken to this evening.

'I'll take those,' he went on, lifting the plate and mug from her hand. 'I want to speak to

Roberto to reassure him that he won't have any more problems in the dining room.' He started walking back towards the door. 'Aren't you off duty now?'

She nodded. There she was being the dutiful nurse again, he thought. She'd handled the emergency situation just as well as he could have. Truth be told, she hadn't really needed him there. Her care and attention to Roberto had obviously been excellent.

It gave him the spur he needed. There was an underlying attraction between them but he still hadn't got to the bottom of what made her tick.

And there still hadn't been the opportunity to talk a little more about her friend. She seemed to get prickly whenever Jill's name was mentioned. Did she really not know what motivated Jill?

He needed to get to know her a little better. Thankfully, she didn't seem to be like her friend at all. And after that night he wanted to see if they could get along together. He wanted her to see the other side of him—away from internet rumours and newspaper headlines.

He needed a chance, outside this environment, to see how she reacted to him. And thanks to

Kevin, their colleague, he knew exactly how to do it.

'Francesca?'

She jumped—she'd obviously been daydreaming. She looked at him a little self-consciously and tucked a loose tendril of hair behind her ear. 'Yes?'

'Ever been to Pisa?'

Her head tilted to the side. 'No.' She smiled curiously at him. 'Why do you ask?'

'Because the ship docks at Livorno tomorrow and if you are free I thought you might want to do some sightseeing with me.'

Whoa. Totally sideswiped. Where had this come from?

'Why Pisa?' she asked suspiciously, raising her eyebrows. 'Why not Florence?' Her brain was racing and she was trying her hardest to act as normally as possible. Both cities were accessible from the port of Livorno and it was usually a pretty even split between the passengers over which city they visited.

He crossed the room and put a hand on her waist, bending his head forward to hers. 'Because a little bird told me that you'd never managed to get there so I thought I might have the pleasure of showing you around.'

As his hand touched her waist she sucked in her breath. His movements were so easy, so casual. Almost as if he touched her that way every day. Was all this awkwardness just in her head?

The 'little bird' must have been Kevin as she'd told him the other day that even though she had done this cruise seven times, she had never managed to see Pisa. It was almost as if he'd read her mind.

'I would love to see Pisa.'

'How about we meet for breakfast tomorrow?' he asked. 'Get the day off to a good start?' There was a twinkle in his eye that made her heart flutter. Was he flirting with her? Or was she acting like some crazy hormonal teenager?

'I'll only meet you if you agree to meet at the Poseidon Lounge and not in the dining room. Who knows what Enzo might do to your food in there.'

He rolled his eyes. 'Doesn't even bear thinking about. Eight o'clock?'

'Eight o'clock is fine.' Francesca picked up her bag and headed to the door.

'Francesca?'

She turned back. 'Yes?'

'You won't need to bring your book. I'll keep you entertained.'

CHAPTER NINE

Hi Jill

Sorry for the delay getting back to you. The ship has been busier than I expected.

Gabriel seems to have settled in fine. He's back here because his father isn't keeping too well. He certainly started off with a splash by rescuing a teenage boy who'd fallen into Venice harbour and was being swept out to sea. His first day was nearly his last as he rescued the boy then knocked himself out on the harbour wall. That's why I had to resuscitate him. Though, at the time, if I'd known who he was I doubt I would have bothered.

He hasn't talked about you, even though I told him how I recognised him. He doesn't say much of anything too personal. His doctoring skills, however, are another story and I've seen some impressive paediatric skills in the last few weeks. He caught a really unusual case in a child that could have resulted in her death if it had been missed.

The women seem to love him—all Italian charm, white teeth and Mediterranean skin. Very different from what I'm used to!

Hope things are going well with you. Have sent you a photo as you requested from one of our crew events.

Francesca

SEND. She sighed and leaned back from the computer. Six composed and deleted emails. There was no point in reading this one over and over like the rest of them. Then she'd just start tweaking it again and again.

And against her better judgement she'd sent the snapshot Jill had requested. If she hadn't it would only have resulted in a whole barrage of emails, so it was better to get it over and done with. Kevin had snapped it the other day when they'd been doing a crew training exercise and the photos had been uploaded to the medical centre computer, so it was easy to access without anyone asking difficult questions.

Would this mean that Jill would reply instantly,

looking for more information about Gabriel? Because right now, Francesca wasn't sure how to answer any queries. She had no idea what was happening between them. All she knew was that *something* was.

And now she'd agreed to spend the day ashore with him.

The fact of the matter was this man was driving her crazy.

The sun was already streaming through her porthole when Francesca woke up. Her stomach gave a little lurch. A whole day with Gabriel. Half of her was dreading it, the other half…

She felt like a teenager going on a first date. Why?

Was it because he looked like an Italian film star? Or was it because she'd spent the last few weeks getting to know him? She'd seen him charm the most rambunctious child. He was thoughtful and kind with patients and their relatives. And every now and then she caught him looking at her through those hooded lids and it made her heart flutter.

There, she'd said it.

There was a definite attraction between them. One that neither of them seemed prepared to act on.

Ever since that night when he'd walked her back to her cabin and kissed her, she'd felt as if she was just waiting for something to happen. The kiss had been the briefest of touches but it had affected her in a way she'd never expected. How had Gabriel got under her skin?

And now she was going to spend the whole day with him…

Why had he asked her? Did he feel something, too? Maybe she was reading too much into it and he was just being courteous to a colleague, offering to show her around an area he was familiar with.

It wasn't like she'd never been kissed before. Actually, she'd been kissed quite a lot. Just not like *that*—and he hadn't even kissed her on the lips. Even when she'd spent time with the playboy doc he hadn't kissed her like that.

She'd had a number of boyfriends over the years but she'd never been broken-hearted when the relationships had ended. Sometimes she had actually felt relief. The truth was that since her

parents had died Francesca had felt totally iso-
lated.

No one had ever filled the gap that they had
left. And nowhere had ever felt like home since.

Travelling had been the ideal way for her to try
and cope. It gave her convenient blasé answers to
difficult questions. *'I don't want to settle down—
I want to see the world.'* No one really knew her
well enough to ask questions about her family.

Australia was just the next port of call on her
long list. After that it would be America—or
maybe Hong Kong. Anywhere but Glasgow.

Her heartbeat quickened as she remembered
the thick envelope inside her bedside cabinet—
currently unopened.

She wasn't quite sure why she hadn't opened it
straight away, even though she seemed to have
been waiting for it for ever. But once she opened
it, it would be time to move on again. And something about the cruise ship was starting to feel
like home.

She showered quickly and dressed in white
Capri pants, a red cotton blouse and some flat
white shoes that would be comfortable to walk
in. It only took a few seconds to pull her hair

back with a clasp—she didn't want to be hot and uncomfortable today. She tossed sunscreen and lip gloss into her bag before picking it up and heading out the door.

Gabriel was sitting in the sunshine at the Poseidon Lounge, waiting for her. The food was served buffet style inside the lounge, which was surrounded by glass on all sides. Although some tables were inside, the majority were out on the deck, where passengers had the chance to eat breakfast in the early morning sun and watch the waves.

'It's kind of ironic, isn't it?'

'What is?'

Gabriel pointed to the sign above his head. 'That they named one of the restaurants after the greatest US disaster movies of all time.'

Francesca smiled. It was the kind of smile that had captured his attention right from the beginning. The kind that spread across her face and right up into her eyes. The kind she gave when she was relaxed, unguarded.

His eyes ran up and down her body. She looked as gorgeous as ever in her white trousers and red shirt, her chestnut curls swept back with a clip and sunglasses perched on top of her head.

'Somehow I don't think they named the restaurant after a movie. It think it was named after the Greek god of the sea.'

Gabriel shrugged. 'Greek. I hear he was a bit of a rogue.'

'Poseidon?'

He nodded.

'And Italians aren't?' She raised her eyebrow as if waiting for him to take the bait. 'I think the expression you're looking for is, *It takes one to know one.*'

She had that little sparkle in her eyes. She grabbed his arm. 'Come on, let's eat. I'm starving.'

They walked through to the buffet and he watched while she piled her plate with scrambled eggs, toast and sausages before adding a pot of tea to the tray she was carrying. She turned around and stretched out her hands to add his plates to her tray.

A frown wrinkled her brow. 'What? That's it?'

He handed over his bowl of muesli as he filled up his coffee cup.

'I'm not a big eater in the morning.' His eyes caught her plate again and glinted with amusement. 'Unlike some other people.'

'I have a feeling I will need all the sustenance I can get,' she said with a smile on her face. She walked back out into the sunshine and sat down at the table.

They had arrived at Livorno at 7:00 a.m. This was the port for Florence and Pisa. Even though it was only a little after eight, the port was bustling with activity. Most of the passengers who were travelling to Florence would be leaving soon. The buses had already congregated near the ship and the tour guides were checking lists with passenger names. Gabriel looked at his watch. They still had plenty of time to eat breakfast. Pisa was closer to the port than Florence and the bus journey much shorter.

There it was again—that glint in her eye. She was in a really good mood this morning. Either that or she'd finally loosened up around him and stopped blaming him for what had happened with her friend.

She took a bite of her toast. 'So—just out of

interest—think we would have got served in Drake's Dining Room this morning?'

Gabriel choked on his coffee. She was surprising him. Her sense of humour was coming out, the one that she only normally revealed to other people. He shook his head. 'I know the captain read the Riot Act to Enzo yesterday so in principle we should be fine. But in reality? I've no intention of setting foot in that dining room in the near future.' He gave a little fake shudder. 'As you said, who knows what he might do to our food?'

'Just as well we came here, then.' Francesca set her coffee cup down on the table and took in a deep breath of sea air. 'I much prefer it here anyway. There's nothing nicer than eating breakfast out on deck.'

Gabriel gazed out onto the dock. The buses laden with passengers heading for Florence had already started to leave. It would probably be best to get going.

'Have you finished?'

Francesca nodded. 'Do you want to go?'

He gestured his head towards the dock. 'We

could catch one of the buses into Pisa. Do you need to get anything from your cabin?'

She shook her head and picked up her bag. 'I'm the kind of girl who travels light. I've got everything I need.'

Just for a second he hesitated, and then he held out his hand towards her. Would she take it? It seemed like the most natural instinct to him, but he didn't want to do anything that made her feel uncomfortable. He wanted to follow her lead.

This was nothing. This was just two colleagues on a day out.

It was harmless. So why was he having thoughts about Francesca that he never had about any other colleague?

Why—every time he closed his eyes—did he relive the feel of her warm body next to his, their lips almost brushing together, the sparks of electricity in the air?

Why did she continually invade his thoughts, no matter what he was doing?

He could see the fleeting expression on her face. As if she was trying to make up her mind.

Then she stretched out her hand and took his, allowing him to pull her up from her seat.

'Ready?'

She was poised right next to his hip. Any other time, any other woman, he would have slid his arm around her waist.

Under any other set of circumstances he would probably have kissed her, too.

But Francesca was different. This was the woman who had spent the first week on board glaring at him. The second week she'd begun to thaw. The third week they'd shared that moment in the corridor. And now? She'd only recently begun to look him in the eye and have normal conversations with him.

He had no idea how she felt. Was she trying to fight the natural attraction between them?

Because he wasn't imagining the chemistry between them. There was definitely something there. They'd both felt it. Especially that night in the Atlantis Bar when he'd walked her back to her cabin.

Those big brown eyes and plump red lips had almost been the death of him. Not to mention the figure-hugging red dress.

The only thing that had stopped him had been the consequences. That—and the tiny niggling question at the back of his mind about her necklace.

Maybe this was nothing to do with Francesca. Maybe this was about the poor choices he'd made in the past when it came to women. Jill, the would-be reporter, and a number of others all more interested in Gabriel Russo the heir to the Russo fortune than Gabriel Russo the person. Every gold-digger under the sun, it seemed, had tried her hand with him. Maybe he should just get over it.

Because in the last few weeks he'd seen or heard nothing to make him suspicious of Francesca. Maybe she was just naturally quite reserved. Closed off to those she didn't know well. Maybe if he could get to the bottom of her lack of confidence at work, he could get to know her a little better. Maybe even enough to…

Time to get the day started. Gabriel grabbed her hand in his and pulled her towards the gangway. He spoke to one of the cruise stewards who pointed them in the direction of the next bus due to leave for Pisa. It was almost full and they grabbed the last two seats together moments before the doors closed. The bus set off and Gabriel turned to face her. 'So what do want to do in Pisa?'

'What do you think?'

He groaned and shook his head. 'No. I am *not* taking a photograph of you pretending to hold up the Leaning Tower!'

She folded her arms across her chest. 'Then I'm not getting out of this bus.'

'You're such a tourist.'

'I know. But that's why I've came here today. I've never seen the Leaning Tower and I hear you can climb up it now, so I definitely want to do that. I don't care how many times you have done it before—you're doing it again today.'

'The Leaning Tower was closed for a spell when I was younger but it's been open for the last few years. We used to spend our summers in Pisa so I've been up it more times than I can count.'

'So, are you going to be a tourist, too, and climb the tower with me? Or are you just going to sit at one of the nearby cafés and wave from down below?'

'Anything else for us to do?'

She leaned back in her seat watching everything speed past. 'No, I just want to be a tourist today. Absolutely no medical dramas. No shopping. But definitely eating. You will buy me lunch today.'

He gave her a mysterious look. 'Ah, I've already made plans for that. But I won't need to buy you lunch.'

She looked at him in surprise. 'Don't even try to pass me off with a cruise-ship sandwich.'

He shook his head. 'No need. My father's cousin has a restaurant near the Piazza Dei Miracoli. Lunch is on him.'

Francesca felt her stomach lurch. 'So I get to meet a member of your family? No wonder they call it the Field of Miracles.'

'What do you mean by that?' He looked bewildered.

'Because no one knows that much about you. You don't give much away. You're a bit of an enigma, to be honest.'

'You mean you haven't read all about me on the internet?'

Her cheeks gave the hint of a flush and she had the good grace to look embarrassed. Part of him felt disappointed. 'Never mind.'

The bus pulled up in a large asphalt car park. The passengers disembarked and the tour guides started to put them into groups. 'Come on,' said Gabriel, 'we don't need to wait for this.'

He clasped her hand again and walked her along next to a high wall. The sun was already beating down and the heat could almost be seen rising from the ground. They walked a few hundred yards before they reached a large archway in the wall. They turned to walk through and Francesca stopped dead. 'Wow!'

There before them stood the Field of Miracles. On the left-hand side were the three white monuments. The sun was reflecting off the white marble, making it glisten in the bright light. The effect was startling.

Gabriel watched Francesca's face in amusement. He had wondered what she would think when she first saw this. Many people were taken aback by the initial glare coming off the buildings. That, along with the fact they were hidden behind the large wall and seemed to appear out of nowhere, made the sight all the more startling.

Gabriel could remember the first time he and his sister had come here. They had fallen in love instantly with the monuments and, because they had family here, had spent many hours playing on the grass in front. He gave her arm a little tug. 'You're blocking people's view,' he whispered as he pulled her to one side.

'Sorry.' She stepped to the left-hand side, nearest to the Baptistery.

'It's just astonishing.' Her eyes were alight with excitement. 'I honestly didn't expect that when we walked around the corner.' She watched the crooked smile that was bending up one corner of his mouth. 'You knew, didn't you?'

'Most people get a surprise when they turn the corner. I wondered what you'd say.'

She fumbled around in her bag to find her camera. 'Let's take some pictures.'

'Let's go and admire the monuments first,' said Gabriel. He stopped in front of one the cafés that lined the right-hand side of the square. 'And let's grab a coffee while we do it.'

'Just a coffee?' quipped Francesca. 'Or do you really plan on feeding me all day?'

He shot her a quick smile and came out of the café two minutes later with two steaming paper cups in his hands. He passed one over to her.

'Here you go, cappuccino with extra chocolate on top.'

'How did you know?'

He tapped the side of his nose. 'I know everything.' He handed over something else, a bag containing a pink box tied with a ribbon. 'Italian chocolates—but save them for later.'

They walked towards the Leaning Tower. 'I guess you want to admire this first,' he said, sweeping his hand towards the impressive structure in front of them.

'No,' she said determinedly. 'I don't just want to admire it, I want to *climb* it. Come on, let's go.' She turned him round and pushed him towards the bell tower. 'Now how many steps are there?'

Gabriel looked at the imposing tower. 'It depends which set of stairs you climb. The south-facing staircase has two hundred and ninety-six; the north-facing staircase has two hundred and ninety-four.'

Francesca gulped. She stood underneath and looked straight upwards at the tower. It really did look as if it could topple over at any moment. She had seen dozens of pictures and news reports about the Leaning Tower but here, seeing it in the flesh, so to speak, was entirely different. She felt as if she could walk over and give it a push with her little finger. 'I should probably know this, but I've forgotten. What made it tilt like this?'

'Shallow foundations, set in weak, unstable subsoil. They tried many ways to stabilise it. They had tons of lead counterweights on the raised end of the base before finally removing soil from underneath. It's supposed to be stable now for at least two hundred years.'

'So it's safe enough to climb?'

'Definitely. Most people book in advance, though. You're usually given a scheduled time to climb the tower.'

Her face fell instantly. 'You're joking, right? Why didn't you tell me this before? You must have known about it.'

There it was again—that vulnerability about her. She looked like a child who had just had her sweeties snatched out of her hand. How could any man resist that?

She was making him see Pisa through a tourist's eyes. She was reminding him how much he used to love being here. Seeing her face as they'd walked through the archway in the wall had made him appreciate his surroundings all the more. What would she think when they reached the top of the Leaning Tower?

Time to find out.

'Because I came prepared.' He pulled two tickets from the back pocket of his jeans as they reached the entrance and stood at the bottom of the winding staircases.

She let out a squeal. 'You rat bag!' And swatted her hands at him. 'Right, that's it.' She put her hand on her hip and looked upwards. 'Tell you what, let's have a race.'

'What?'

'You climb one staircase and I'll climb the other. I'll race you to the top. Loser has to pay a forfeit.'

'What kind of forfeit?'

'Whatever the winner decides.'

'I like that,' he said. 'I'm sure I could think of something.'

Francesca took their paper cups to throw in the nearby rubbish bin. In an instant Gabriel had turned and started sprinting up the steps.

Francesca was caught off guard by his quick getaway and dashed to keep up. She had been an excellent sprinter at school and was sure she could outrun him. Her heart was racing as she pounded up the uneven stairs, her legs thumping. She darted to one side to avoid some sightseers who had stopped on the third floor. She heard a yell from the other side of the tower and grinned to herself as she realised Gabriel must have run into some people.

Starting to pant for breath, she continued to charge up the steps, hearing the muttered apologies from the other side of the tower. Her legs were feeling heavy; running up stairs was definitely harder work than sprinting around a racetrack. By the time she reached the seventh floor she could feel the sweat trickling down her back in the warm air. Her face was flushed and her breathing ragged.

With a final spurt she dashed out towards the balcony that looked over the square. Gabriel was standing with his back to her, pretending to be nonchalant, as if he had been waiting for her for a while. She gasped her way over towards him, thudding her hands on the balcony. Although he looked incredibly sexy in his jeans and T-shirt, the small beads of perspiration on his forehead gave away his recent exertions.

'How on earth did you manage to beat me?' she panted. 'I can't believe it'.

He gave her a wide grin. 'What took you so long?'

She slapped his arm in frustration. 'I heard you banging into people on the way up. I was sure I was ahead of you.'

Her heart was thudding rapidly in her chest, but her breathing had started to slow. Gabriel leaned across and pulled her over to one side.

They stood together, looking out over the Field of Miracles. A welcome gentle wind was rippling against them. She leaned forward, looking down at the people in the square. 'This is a beautiful place, Gabriel. You were so lucky getting to spend time here as a child.' She wrinkled her nose, 'Rainy summers in Glasgow weren't quite the same.'

His arm brushed against hers as he leaned next to her. 'I don't think I appreciated it at the time. Everything about it seemed so ordinary. I thought all families did this. It's not till you go away and see the world from another perspective that you realise the importance of what's still at home.'

The words seemed so straightforward but there was a weight beneath them. What did he mean? She turned to face him, leaning back against the railing. 'So how come you spent your summers here when you lived in Venice?'

His eyes lowered, as if he was trying to figure out how to answer what should be a straightforward question. 'Things changed in our family. My mother...' he hesitated '...needed a little space. The summers were long and we had family here in Pisa. My sister and I were delighted to come and spend our summers with our uncle and our cousins.'

So much unsaid. Everybody had secrets—she knew that better than anyone. But what had happened in Gabriel's family? What about the tragedy referred to on the internet search engine? She hadn't read any of those articles.

It would be intrusive to just come right out and ask. But curiosity was killing her. Time to try another tactic. 'So what about Venice? How is your father doing?'

He shrugged. '*Not what the doctors tell him* would be the most appropriate answer.'

'Isn't that the same as most folks?'

He sighed. 'My father is a law unto himself. I'm supposed to be taking over some of the day-to-day things for him—anything I can do electronically—to try and relieve the pressure. Trouble is, Dad just finds something else to do.'

She gave him a smile. 'Sometimes parents are worse than children.' Something curled inside her stomach, sending a lump to her throat.

Gabriel had moved a little closer, reaching up and catching a curl that had escaped from her clip. His fingers brushed her cheek as he tucked the curl behind her ear. His eyes had intensity she hadn't seen before. 'So what's your story, Francesca Cruz?' His body moved closer to hers as some people edged past them.

She could feel the heat pressing against her, but she didn't want to step away. It didn't feel intrusive. It felt natural. It felt comfortable. His other hand settled at the side of her waist.

'I don't know what you mean,' she whispered.

Then he moved even closer, his chest pressing against hers. 'You're one of the best nurses I've worked with, Francesca. Everyone in the team thinks really highly of you. But you seem to be the only person that doesn't think that. What's going on?'

She took a deep breath. If she told him the truth he would hate her. If she told him how she'd nearly sent Carly Glencross away he would be horrified.

She couldn't do that. She couldn't tell him about her dad. She couldn't tell him she'd missed all the signs that could have indicated how low he'd been feeling.

Gabriel's breath was tickling her cheek. She was lost in those dark brown eyes. She didn't want to do anything to spoil this.

'What about our forfeit?' she whispered, a smile creeping across her face.

'Would you like to decide what your forfeit is, or should I?' His voice was husky, the implication clear.

She met his gaze and her stomach tightened. There was no way her heart was going to stop thudding now. At the top of the bell tower the light breeze cooled their heated skin. The beauty of Cathedral Square was just beneath them, but neither of them seemed to notice. He raised his fingers and captured another little chestnut curl that had stuck on her damp skin. He wound it round his finger slowly, never taking his eyes from hers. 'I think we might both have decided the same thing.'

She couldn't move. She couldn't breathe.

His lips bent to meet hers. His kiss was electrifying, the lightest, most delicate of touches. Nothing more, nothing less. With very little pressure his mouth teased the edges of hers. His hand brushed gently along her cheek, settling behind her ear and cradling her head in his hand. The kiss deepened slightly, the pressure increasing as he pushed forward then pulled away. Her first instinct was to grab him. To want more from this kiss. But he released his lips from hers and pressed his forehead against hers. It was perfect.

Their first proper kiss on top of one of the most famous monuments in the world. It could have been a moment from a movie. He might have kissed her outside her cabin. The air had been electric and atmosphere heavy, but it could never have matched this moment. A fleeting brush of his lips on her ear could never compare with this. She took a deep breath and stepped backwards.

He smiled at her, a thousand unspoken thoughts in his eyes. A promise of something else. Something for later.

Because she didn't need anything else right now. Her lips were tingling, the taste of him still there. The scent in her nostrils was that of his distinctive aftershave. The back of her head could still feel the warmth from his hand.

She'd thought everything about Gabriel would feel wrong. But it didn't. It felt very right.

A crowd of voices broke the silence seconds later as a horde of tourists reached the top of the stairs and joined them on the balcony, oblivious to what they had just interrupted.

Gabriel moved over to let some of them past. His hand rested on Francesca's waist. 'Do you want to take some photographs?' he asked, the lazy smile appearing on his face.

Francesca nodded. She wanted to capture this moment. She wanted to remember this. She pulled out her camera and was immediately accosted by a small grey-haired woman.

'Oh, let me, dear,' she said, grabbing the cam-

era from Francesca's hand. 'You make a beautiful couple.'

Francesca looked over at him. Would he want
to capture the moment, too? The enthusiastic
woman gave them a prod to push them together
again.

'Come on, then—give us a smile.'

They stepped together and both gave a smile.
Gabriel's arm was still around her waist and he
pulled her closer, nestling her beneath the crook
of his arm. Her hand naturally lifted and rested
on his firm chest. He smiled at her again, as if
still reliving their secret moment.

Click.

'Perfect!'

The woman handed the camera back and wandered off.

Francesca felt her shoulders ease. She looked
back over the balcony. 'Can we visit the *Duomo*?'

'Anything you want, Francesca.' His words
sounded so simple, but she understood the hidden meaning. He was waiting for her lead.

'Great.' She turned and headed back down
the winding staircase. It was becoming hotter
now and getting busier. They walked across the

crowded square towards the *Duomo*, the medieval cathedral at the heart of the square, his hand loosely grasping hers.

This felt different from this morning. Taking his hand, this morning had been a stepping stone. A starting point. What now?

An instant quiet fell on them as they stepped from the hot and bustling square through the massive bronze doors into the cooler air and hushed tones of the cathedral. Although it was filled with numerous tourists, there was a respectful silence and tranquil feeling inside. Francesca gave a little shudder as her body adjusted to the rapid change in temperature. The gorgeous gold-decorated ceiling gave a feeling of opulence and wealth, as did the decorated mosaics and the carved marble panels showing dramatic scenes from the New Testament.

Gabriel calmly kept her hand in his and walked with her in silence around the statues and elaborately carved pulpit. She was grateful for that silence. Even though she was wandering amongst some of the most beautiful artefacts in the world, Francesca felt as if she could hardly concentrate.

She was conscious of him at her side. Of the dark curling hairs on his arm brushing against hers.

They had finished walking around the cathedral and had reached the bronze doors again. 'Are you ready for lunch yet?'

She gave a little nod. She was beginning to feel more relaxed and calm again. Lunch might be the perfect time to get to know the man she'd kissed a little better. They walked across the square and down a side street towards an Italian restaurant. Gabriel stopped just as they were about to enter the dark wood doors.

He shot her a smile. 'Prepare yourself,' he muttered as he pushed open the door.

Four hours later they stepped back out of the restaurant.

Gabriel had the noisiest and most welcoming family she'd ever met. The food and company had been delicious. The smells alone had been fantastic.

Her head was reeling. She'd barely caught a word of the rapid Italian. Her basic Italian was passable but so many regions of Italy had dialects and she struggled to follow the fast-paced words.

Gabriel had flowed back into his native language with no hesitation whatsoever. His grasp of English was impeccable and she'd almost forgotten it wasn't his first language. But Gabriel, ever the gentleman, had obviously sensed her unease and had stopped time and time again to include her in the conversation.

Seeing the obvious affection he felt for his family had sent little pangs straight to her heart. It was at times like this she missed her mum and dad more than words could say. It made her realise what she'd lost.

'Francesca?'

The voice was a whisper in her ear, his warm hand touching her waist.

'I've something to ask you.'

A little shiver went down her spine. There was something about the way he was looking at her, the way he was touching her. All of a sudden her heart was beating furiously in her chest. Her breath seemed to have caught in her throat. They'd had a perfect day. Was it about to get better? Or was he going to spoil it? She held her breath.

'Want to do this again?'

CHAPTER TEN

'WHAT you doing, gorgeous?'

The words danced over her skin like the warm afternoon sun. She was standing on the adults-only sunbathing deck again. But instead of hiding inside a pod and reading, she was leaning over the rail towards the swimming pool underneath, watching the children play with the entertainers.

She took a sip from her long, cool drink as she turned to face him. 'I like watching the kids. I like watching people who don't seem to have a care in the world.'

She wondered what he'd say as a frown seemed to hover around his brow. The guy was a paediatrician, surely he didn't have an aversion to kids?

He leaned on the rail next to her. 'Families,' he muttered quietly as his eyes swept over the scene below.

There was a whole host of children dancing in

the sun with the entertainers. A younger bunch was in the paddling pool, throwing balls back and forwards. Families of all shapes and descriptions were scattered around the loungers next to the pool.

Francesca laughed as one toddler dumped her ice-cream cone onto her brother's back. He screamed at the top of his voice and ran away.

'I should go down there and talk about sunscreen. Some of those kids look red already.'

She gave him a sharp nudge. 'Stop thinking like a doctor, Gabriel, and start thinking like a normal person and have some fun.'

She couldn't see his eyes as they were hidden behind designer sunglasses. Just like the part of him he kept hidden from her.

But, then, they were both a little guilty of that.

'I like your family. Your father's cousin and his family were great. Think we can go back and visit again? The food in their restaurant was amazing.'

He gave the slightest nod. 'If only the rest of the family was like that.'

'What do you mean?' She pushed her sunglasses up onto her head. 'Aren't you and your dad close? I thought you were back to help him?'

She hoped it sounded like a casual enquiry with no ulterior motive. He'd hardly said a word about his mother or his father. He leaned further over the rail, focusing on the people below.

A classic avoidance tactic. One she'd used herself.

'Gabriel?'

She wasn't going to let this go. She'd shared a kiss with this man. Surely she was entitled to know a little bit more?

'I do what I can at night online. My sister is helping with the day-to-day running of things.'

'Your sister?' She could feel her eyebrows rise. He had barely even mentioned her before.

There was the tiniest moment's hesitation. 'Sofia could run my father's printing company with her eyes shut. She eats, breathes and sleeps the business. Whereas I...' His voice drifted off. 'But she's a girl—that's the problem.'

Francesca felt herself pull back a little. 'Is your father really that old-fashioned? In this day and age?'

She couldn't read him. She couldn't see his eyes at all and it was driving her crazy.

He shrugged, his arm curving around her waist. 'It's complicated,' he said as he bent towards her for a kiss, pressing his body up next to hers. A smile was starting to flicker across his face as if he had other, more pressing things on his mind.

'All family business is complicated,' she said as her arms crept around his neck and she lost herself in his kiss.

Whatever it was, it could wait.

The next two weeks passed by in a blur of ports, beautiful cities, sexy sightseeing and crackling electricity.

And, of course, passengers.

Sunburn and blistering seemed to be the common complaint amongst the children on board, parents misjudging the strength of the Mediterranean sun. For the older patients the trend seemed to be fractured wrists, with falls from the tour buses, slips on the open-air decks and tumbles on the stairwells.

But for Francesca and Gabriel all this was just background noise.

It seemed only natural that when they were apart they would seek each other out. If they weren't working together they were eating together, visiting ancient monuments or watching the entertainment.

The electricity between them seemed to be gaining momentum with every second they spent together.

He'd kissed her again, of course. Each one more tempting than the last. The increasing intensity was driving her crazy. It seemed only natural that things would progress between them. The only question was when. The lack of privacy on the cruise ship was definitely restricting their activities.

But, tonight, for the first time in two weeks, they were finally on call together.

'What are you doing, Gabriel?'

He sighed and leaned back in his chair. The rest of the lights in the medical centre were off and his face was lit up by the computer screen in front of him. 'I'm just typing up some notes for a patient I've just visited.'

'Anyone I know?'

He looked tired and he ran his hand through

his hair. He handed her some notes. 'I don't think you've met him. Jackson King, seventy. Chest infection.' He ran his fingers through his dark hair, as if contemplating his thoughts. 'I should probably put him off at the next port but he's waited a year for this cruise and, to be honest, I don't think he'll make another. I might bring him down and try him on some IV antibiotics next.'

Francesca could feel herself getting flustered. In the past she'd dealt with lots of patients who had died. It was part of the element of being a nurse.

But since she'd lost her dad she found herself getting emotional and irrational about these sorts of things. She'd made a conscious decision to try and take herself out of these scenarios and cruise-ship nursing had been a pretty safe bet.

Most passengers who became unwell were transferred off the ship. It was only in really rare and unfortunate conditions that someone died on board.

Nothing like that had ever happened since Francesca had joined the crew.

A wave of fear swept over her body. 'Is it serious? Do you think he's going to die on board?'

She saw him bite at his bottom lip, his dark eyes fixed on hers. 'Hopefully not. I'd hate to put him off the ship and dump him into a local hospital if all they're going to do is put on him IV antibiotics for a few days and give him oxygen—we can do that here.'

'But maybe that's not in his best interests.' She could feel herself starting to twitter. 'I mean, we may have an X-ray machine but sometimes people are better off in a hospital. We can't deliver the kind of care he might need in here. We could ventilate someone for a few hours at most. And if he reached that stage, it would be even more risky to transfer him. I think it's best if you put him off at the next port, Gabriel.'

Gabriel reached over and took her hand. 'Sit down, Francesca.' His voice was calm but firm. He pulled her over towards the chair next to him. He was looking at her as if she had just sprouted horns.

'Wanna tell me what's going on?'

Her skin felt jittery, the tiny hairs on her arms standing on end. Her brain was working ten to the dozen, she was agitated and she couldn't hide it.

'It's not that I'm saying I can't look after him because obviously I could.' She swept her arm around the state-of-the-art treatment room. 'But it's best for the crew if we don't really have patients overnight. It puts extra pressure on us that we don't need. And we don't have everything we need here.'

He was staring at her with those big brown eyes. She could practically read his thoughts and it wasn't helping.

The *Silver Whisper* had every bit of equipment they could possibly need for a man with a chest infection. An X-ray machine to determine the extent of the infection, IV antibiotics to treat the infection expertly and efficiently, oxygen supplies, monitoring equipment, and an emergency ventilator if needed.

At least once a week they had someone who needed to stay in the medical centre overnight and be monitored. It was part and parcel of the job.

'What's the worst that could happen?' His voice was deep and even, perfectly controlled.

Silence hung in the air. There was the slightest rise of Gabriel's eyebrows.

Francesca could feel her heart thump against her chest. She couldn't breathe. Her chest was tight. She was struggling to pull in air.

She couldn't focus. She kept seeing her father's body sitting in front of her. The terrible colour and tone of his skin. That horrible deathly tinge of grey. It made her want to be sick.

All her nursing life she'd dealt with dead bodies. From the very old to the heartbreaking very young. She'd always treated them with reverence and respect, almost as if they had been members of her own family.

But the cold, harsh jolt of reality had been a terrible experience for her. She couldn't face it. She didn't think she could deal with a dead body again.

Everything had changed now.

'I really don't want to be around someone who's about to die,' she blurted out.

Gabriel was more than a little surprised by her reaction. She was freaking out. His normally calm, capable nurse had turned into a jittery wreck. Her hands were flapping all over the place, she was pacing up and down, talking nineteen to the dozen. What was this about?

She was a nurse. She was used to dealing with death. What on earth was wrong?

She'd helped pull him from the water and resuscitated him. Essentially, until she'd put her hands on his chest, he'd been dead. Until she'd given him mouth to mouth he hadn't been going to breathe again.

But she obviously wasn't thinking like that. This was something different. Her actions in an emergency were automatic—without thought. This was something else entirely.

He stood up and put his hands on her shoulders.

'Francesca, calm down.' She wasn't listening, she was still ranting. 'Francesca.' The volume of his voice increased, bringing her to a halt. There were tears glistening in her eyes, threatening to spill down her cheeks at any second.

This wasn't a normal reaction. This wasn't a professional response.

This was personal.

He guided her into the chair once again and knelt in front of her. The time his voice was quiet, almost a whisper. 'What is it, Francesca? What happened?'

Her shoulders started to shake and the dam burst. Whatever had been threatening to erupt inside her had just taken over. He put his arm around her shoulder as she sobbed, rubbing her back and letting her rest her head on his shoulder.

'My dad,' she sobbed. 'It was my dad.'

He ran his hand through her tangled hair, smoothing it down with the palm of his hand. The shoulder of his shirt was sodden with her tears but he didn't care. At last he was getting to the bottom of what was wrong with her.

'What happened to your dad, Francesca?' She hardly mentioned her parents. It had always seemed like a sensitive area. He knew both her parents had died, but had no idea of the circumstances. When he'd made tentative queries with the other staff, none of them seemed to know, either.

'I missed the signs. I should have known. I should have paid more attention.' He took a sharp intake of breath. Had her father died of a chest infection?

But Francesca wasn't finished. 'If I'd just understood how lonely he was then I would have known to pay more attention.' No. This didn't sound like a chest infection. This sounded like something else entirely.

Pieces of the jigsaw puzzle started to slot into place. 'How long ago did your mum die, Francesca?'

'Five years. I left London to come back home and help my dad.' Her eyes lifted to meet his. 'It was hard for us both and he was depressed after it.' She shook her head. 'But he was better, at least I *thought* he was getting better. He'd started to go out more, take care of his appearance. I thought the depression had lifted. I never would have left him alone otherwise. He was all I had left.' She doubled over, her body racked with sobs again and her head in her hands.

Gabriel took a deep breath. Everything was fitting together. 'Did your father commit suicide, Francesca?'

Through her sobs she nodded.

Everything seemed crystal clear to him now. That's why she struggled at work. That's why she didn't trust her instincts.

She'd missed something in the person who had

meant the most to her in the world. She was crippled by guilt. Anyone would be.

He understood it well. He'd only been a child when Dante had died, but that didn't stop the feelings of guilt. That he should have known something was wrong with his brother. He should have tried to help his mother more. He should have chased after that obnoxious doctor when he'd left the house saying Dante would be fine in a few days.

He pushed a stray tendril of hair behind her ear and put his fingers under her chin, lifting her face to his.

'That wasn't your fault, Francesca.'

'Then whose fault was it?' Her voice was angry. She needed to vent.

He ran his hand along the length of her arm, stroking her skin. 'Francesca, often we can't see things in those we love most. You thought your dad was getting better. You were probably feeling relieved.' He shook his head, 'It's not till after the fact that you get to examine things. You must know by now that often people who are depressed seem to have a spell when they pick up, make improvements, and then something like this happens.' He clasped her hands in his.

'It's not your fault. This could never be your fault. I didn't know your father, or know his reasons. But he was an adult, Francesca. The decision to do that was his. It doesn't take away from how much he must have loved you.'

She was shaking her head slowly. 'But he was my responsibility, Gabriel. *Mine*. No one else's. I should have seen the signs.'

Gabriel nodded. 'I know that's what you believe. And I know that's what has been affecting your work. You think you've lost your instincts, you think you made a mistake.' Her eyes widened. 'But you haven't, Francesca. You're one of the most competent nurses I've ever worked with. And your instincts are spot on.'

A single tear dripped down her cheek and she lowered her gaze. 'I'm not, Gabriel. You have no idea,' she whispered.

'You're a nurse. I know you're scared. But you're going to have to learn to deal with death again. In this job, we have to be prepared. We have to be prepared for anything.'

He rubbed his hand over the top of hers. 'I'm

going to tell you something that hardly anyone knows about me.'

Gabriel drew in a long, slow breath. He had to tell her. He had to share with her. She had to know she wasn't alone in feeling she'd let down her family. He had to be honest with her.

'I don't just have a sister.'

She tilted her head and looked confused.

'I used to have a brother, too. Dante died when he was a baby. I was six. Dante had meningitis—except we didn't know it at the time. My mother called for the doctor, but he was tired or drunk—or both. He was in and out of our house in less than five minutes, saying Dante would be fine in a few days. But my mother *knew*. My mother knew something was wrong. We all did. I've never heard a cry like that before. And by the time we took him to the hospital a few hours later it was too late.'

'Oh, Gabriel. I'm so sorry.' Her hand reached up and stroked the side of his face.

He caught her hand back in his. 'A mother's instinct is never wrong. It's the most valuable lesson I've ever learned. So I *know*, Francesca. I understand what it feels like to miss something in a family member. To question every day if there was something else—something different—you could have done.' He held her hand next to his chest. 'I understand in a way that other people can't. Because I feel guilty, too.'

Her reaction was instantaneous. She shook her head. 'But that's ridiculous. You were a child. You couldn't have done anything to save your brother. You know how it is with meningitis. It's so quick. It's so deadly. Even with all the technology in the world, we still can't save everyone.'

He pressed her hand closer to his chest. 'It doesn't matter what the logical explanation is, Francesca. It doesn't change what I feel in here. Just like it doesn't change what you feel in here.' He reached over and pressed his hand over her heart. He felt her pull her breath into her lungs, holding it in place, while she contemplated his words.

'Because our family was well known in Italy it was all over the press. Everywhere we went there were reporters following us, photographers snapping pictures. My mother was fragile enough as it was.' He shook his head. 'To add that into the equation…'

Now she would understand. He could see the realisation dawning on her of why he hadn't wanted any press intrusion about the incident in Venice harbour. Her hand pushed against him even more.

He was kneeling on the floor in front of her. In the dimly lit room she was beautiful, her eyes wide, her vulnerability shining through.

Did she know just how irresistible she was? Did she know how many times he'd wanted to kiss her? How much he wanted her?

'Sometimes we just need somebody.'

Her eyes met his. Dark brown, melting pools of chocolate.

'I need you, Gabriel.' Her voice had changed. This time there was no tremor—no vulnerability. This time it had a very determined edge.

Did she mean what he thought she did?

'Francesca?'

She moved from her chair. A decisive movement, kneeling on the floor to face him.

They were almost nose to nose, just inches apart.

She lifted her hand to touch the side of his face and ran her fingers through his hair.

He caught her hand in his. 'Are you sure?' The atmosphere in the room was so tense he could barely growl the words out.

'I'm sure.' There was no shred of doubt in her voice.

'Then not here.' It was all he could do not to push her onto the floor or up against the wall in the medical centre. But no matter how much he wanted her, he couldn't do that.

Anyone could walk in here at any time.

For Francesca he wanted uninterrupted time and pleasure.

He pulled her towards the door, striding down the quiet corridors of the ship towards his cabin—the two-minute journey had never seemed so long—fumbling in his pocket to find his card to open the door.

She could feel the electricity in the air between them; it felt as if any minute now a million fireworks could go off in a dazzling multicoloured display.

As the door sprung open she found herself slammed up against the wall, her hands above her head. His mouth was on hers in a second. Warm, scorching heat. His tongue probing, pressing her lips apart. This was no gentle kiss like the one on top of the Leaning Tower. This was pure passion.

She pressed herself against the blazing heat of his body, feeling his instant hardness across her taut stomach. Her fingers started tugging at the buttons on his shirt, struggling to unfasten them quickly. Her heart was thundering in her chest and her head was spinning. He pulled her over towards his bed and they crashed onto the mattress together. 'Tell me this is what you want,' he growled.

He bent forward and started leaving a trail of kisses behind her left ear, down the delicate, ticklish skin at the side of her neck and across her shoulder bone, carrying on downwards until he reached the skin between her breasts. Francesca squirmed in delight, feeling his breath on her electrified skin as he tantalised and teased her with his lighter-than-air kisses.

He reached up and wound his fingers around the strap of her bra, pulling it down roughly to release her swollen breast from the confines of her underwear. A wicked grin came over his face and he leaned over and flicked his tongue over the prize.

She groaned out aloud and her body reacted instinctively to his, arching her back towards him, thrusting her nipple further into his mouth. He devoured her endlessly before rising, brushing a kiss across her lips, and started his trail of butterfly kisses again under her other ear. She could barely stand the tension as she could feel the first involuntary tremors of arousal in her body. His hand lifted to move her second strap and release the other breast from its confines.

She pulled his shirt apart, pushing it down over his shoulders. She wanted to see him. She wanted to feel him. She didn't want anything between them.

His other hand wound its way downwards and inside her silk panties to find her moistness, stroking it with expert fingers. Francesca could stand the torment no longer. In his position astride her she could see and feel his erection brushing against her stomach.

'Don't play games with me, Gabriel,' she

breathed. She wasn't waiting a second longer as she tugged at his trousers.

His reaction was instant as he fumbled from the bed and threw his clothes across the floor. He stopped for a few seconds. There was a rustle of a wrapper before he was poised above her again.

Francesca used that time to push her silk panties over her legs to join his clothes in the puddle next to the bed.

Within seconds he was back on top of her on the bed. He gently pressed the length of his naked body next to hers. She responded immediately by opening her legs and winding them around his waist. 'Now, Gabriel,' she gasped. He was poised above her again and he hesitated, still waiting for her lead.

'Are you sure?'

'Come on, Gabriel.' She grabbed his shoulders. There was no doubt in her mind. If he stopped now, she would kill him.

She tilted her hips up towards him. Nothing else mattered. Nothing but right now and this moment. Nothing had ever felt this good.

He entered her in one powerful thrust sending shockwaves shooting through her body. The pressure increased with each stroke as his momentum increased, the tide of passion rising quickly. She wound her legs tighter around his body to pull him deeper into her as the first waves of ecstasy throbbed through her.

Making love had never felt like this before—everything about it was different. She'd never felt this kind of connection before.

Maybe it was because of what she'd shared with him? And what he'd shared with her?

She had never been able to do that before—to talk about her father and what he'd done.

She'd seen the hurt in his eyes, just as he must have seen it in hers. It had given her this—the first time she'd felt truly connected to a man.

She was losing control. The sensations were sweeping over. Taking her to the place she wanted to go. Gabriel touched her face and whispered in her ear. Words of emotion. Words of tenderness. Words of passion.

And she let go.

She glanced at the clock on his bedside table; it was after midnight and Gabriel was already sleeping. She wondered what it would be like to wake up every morning next to this gorgeous man. A man who had spent the last few hours treating her as though she was the most important thing on earth.

She wondered what it would be like to share his bed every night.

The release of endorphins was obviously making her crazy because, in her head, she was picturing two dark-eyed children playing outside a beautiful house, with Gabriel and herself standing in the garden, watching.

Clearly, she was losing her mind.

She had never allowed herself to formulate dreams like this—she was so used to being alone. But Gabriel had evoked feelings in her that she could never have hoped for. His heat was enveloping her now like a warm blanket and ripples of fatigue were tugging at her. She dug her head into the feather pillow. This bed was much more comfortable than hers; she could get use to this.

It was almost as if a huge weight had been lifted off her shoulders. She'd hardly ever spoke to anyone about this.

She'd never known talking about it could have this effect.

But it wasn't just what she'd said. It was what *he'd* said that mattered.

He'd shared with her about his brother. How hard must it have been to dig up all those childhood emotions and memories? No wonder he never spoke about it. The pain had been etched on his heart, just like it was on hers.

Had she finally met someone who could understand? Really understand what this felt like?

Someone she could finally share with? Someone to take the aching feeling of loneliness away?

That could be too good to be true.

Her plans drifted through her mind, like feathers in the wind scattering aimlessly around.

Her letter from Australia? It might never be opened.

CHAPTER ELEVEN

TIME was beginning to drift for Francesca. Her letter had sat unopened in her bedside cabinet for weeks.

She'd been very busy. Busy spending every moment with Gabriel.

Today they were on duty. The boat had docked at Mykonos in Greece, with most of the passengers visiting the nearby town with its maze of tiny streets and whitewashed-steps lanes. Things had been quiet.

But that was about to change.

They heard a cry from the corridor. It was the most distinctive cry she'd ever heard.

Gabriel was on his feet in an instant, not waiting for the patient to reach the medical centre but striding down the corridor at lightning speed.

Seconds later he returned with a toddler in his arms. The scream was like nothing Francesca had ever experienced before. Something was really wrong.

Gabriel laid the little one down on the one of the examination trolleys, listening as the parents joined him, both talking at once.

Francesca picked up fragments of the conversation as she connected the little one to a monitor. 'Temperature…fretful…not drinking… screaming.'

Gabriel was sounding his chest. Francesca lifted the tympanic thermometer and put it in his ear. 'High temp, Gabriel. Thirty-nine point eight.'

She lifted a nearby chart and touched the arm of the child's mother. 'Excuse me, what's your son's name?' In the speed and confusion she hadn't heard it.

'It's Jake. His name is Jake. Jake Peterson.'

Francesca nodded. 'Date of birth?' She wrote down the details; he was only fourteen months old. She watched as Gabriel finished sounding his chest, checked his blood pressure and checked his ears, nose and throat.

'He had an ear infection last week,' said his mother anxiously. 'He had antibiotics but I'm not sure if they've worked. We gave him paracetamol but his temperature won't come down. He won't drink. He's been vomiting.'

Francesca was still watching Gabriel. Was that a tremor in his hands? Did he suspect what she thought he did?

On autopilot she reached over and touched Jake's hands and feet. While his body temperature was high, his hands and feet were distinctly cold. An indicator of meningitis in children.

She gave Gabriel a little nod. He understood instantly. He took a few more moments, placing his hand behind Jake's head and lifting it while keeping his other hand on Jake's chest. The movement caused an involuntary reaction in Jake, flexing his hips and knees. 'Positive Brudzinki's.' He glanced over at Francesca. And she could see it.

The pain written all over his face.

Was Jake the same age that Dante had been?

He pointed to the phone on the nearby wall. 'Phone the captain, tell him we have a medical emergency. Tell him not to leave port.'

Francesca glanced at her watch. The ship was due to leave Mykonos in the next few minutes.

The engines had already started up and the anchor probably lifted. It was vital they stop this. Every minute in a meningitis case counted. An emergency sea evacuation would take up precious time. She spoke swiftly and quietly then hung up the phone. 'It's done.'

'What's happening? What's wrong with Jake?'

Gabriel put his hand on Jake's mums shoulder. 'Jake is showing signs of meningitis.'

She looked aghast. 'No. He can't be. He's had those vaccinations. He can't have meningitis.'

Her hand stroked the head of her son lying on the bed. The screaming had stopped. He was floppy and lethargic. His heart beating too fast, his colour pale.

Gabriel appeared calm. But she could hear it. The tiny tremor in his voice. The absolute control he was exercising over himself.

'Unfortunately there are lots of different types of meningitis. The vaccines only protect against the most common. Jake has obviously picked up another type. We won't be sure which type until we can do some tests, but in the meantime I'm going to give him some intravenous antibiotics.'

The woman gripped Gabriel's arm fiercely.

'What if you're wrong? What if it's not meningitis? Don't you need to do that horrible test on Jake to find out? The needle in his back?'

Gabriel shook his head. 'There's no time. I'm going to give him antibiotics and arrange immediate transfer to a children's hospital. He'll need some steroids, too. We can't wait. We have to act now.'

He was moving across the treatment room, opening cupboards, obviously searching for what he needed.

'What IV antibiotics have we got?'

Francesca was at his side in an instant. She glanced at the small, pale child over her shoulder. 'What do you want?'

'Vancomycin.'

She shook her head. They only had the most basic antibiotics on board. 'Benzylpenicillin or cefotaxime, then.'

'We've got both of them.' She waited while he scribbled his prescriptions.

'I'll take some bloods and insert the IV cannula while you make up the loading drugs.'

She nodded and got to work quickly. This must be his worst nightmare. She couldn't imagine how he must be feeling. Outwardly he seemed cool, calm and collected. An experienced paediatrician dealing with something he must have seen before.

Jake's mother had started to cry. 'But he doesn't even have a rash...'

Francesca touched her arm as she hung the bag of fluids up and ran the infusion through the IV line. 'It's probably best that he doesn't. A rash is a really critical sign of meningitis. The sooner we get these started the better.'

It had only taken Gabriel a few seconds to collect the blood samples and insert the cannula.

Francesca joined up the IV and set the electronic pump. It was important that these antibiotics were delivered as quickly and as safely as possible. She handed Gabriel a scrap of paper.

'Here are the nearest hospital's contact details. I'm not sure who the paediatrician is there.'

He nodded and walked swiftly over to his office, leaving the door open so he could continue to observe Jake as he made the call.

It was all over in a few minutes. 'Ambulance should be here soon. They're sending a doctor to do the transfer.'

Francesca started a new set of observations on Jake. There was no change. No improvement, no deterioration. Gabriel never left his side, writing his notes at the bedside and talking calmly and quietly to Jake's parents.

Ten minutes later the phone in the medical centre rang to say the ambulance was at port side. There had been no time to make any alternative arrangements, and the family's luggage was still on board as the stewards hadn't had enough time to pack up their cabin.

One of the pursers brought the family their passports and money from the safe in their cabin and promised to arrange the transport for their luggage. It was as much as they could do.

For Jake, time was of the essence. Everything else would have to wait.

Ten minutes later Jake and his parents were in the back of the ambulance, speeding off to the local children's unit in Mykonos.

Francesca and Gabriel walked back up the stairs to the medical centre in silence. She was watching him carefully.

He was clenching his fists and his jaw was firmly set. It was clear his frustration and anger was building. He strode ahead swiftly and she jumped as something crashed off the wall in front of her.

'We need to get better antibiotics in here! That child could have died!'

She froze. She'd never seen him like this before. His anger was frightening, even though it wasn't directed at her.

She turned to face him. 'You did a good job, Gabriel,' she said quietly. It was a calm, measured response, hopefully one that would permeate across to him.

'What if we'd been at sea?' He was pacing now. His anger clearly had not abated. His hands were shaking.

She walked over to the worktop in front of her and started clearing up the remnants from earlier. Discarded vials, packaging from the IV line, the plastic cover for the bag of saline.

She'd no idea how to handle this. She knew he was angry. She knew he was frustrated. But the anger spike made her recoil.

Was that wrong? Shouldn't she be trying to support him, the way he had her?

He was a wreck.

Francesca walked across the room towards him.

She placed a hand gently on his arm. 'But he didn't, Gabriel.' She could feel a tremor in his arms.

It was her turn. He was one of the finest doctors she'd ever worked with.

If she hadn't known about his brother she would never have understood his reaction.

But he'd shared with her.

He'd told her something he didn't share with anyone and she loved him for it.

There. The words had finally formed in her head.

The man she'd started out hating was the man she'd finally bared her soul to. The one who was stealing a place in her heart.

She lifted her hands up onto his shoulders. 'You did good, Gabriel.'

'If we'd been at sea you would have started the antibiotics and the steroids and arranged the quickest air ambulance you could.' She paused, watching the frown that puckered his handsome face.

'Haven't you had to deal with a child with meningitis before?' It almost felt disloyal to ask the question. But she had to know. He was paediatrician. Surely he dealt with this before?

His reply was abrupt, snappy. 'Of course I've dealt with kids with meningitis. Just not in the middle of the sea before. I've always had the equipment and people around me that I needed.'

His words stung. Did he think she wasn't good enough to deal with a severely sick child? And they weren't in the middle of the sea. They were in a port, next to a reliable and capable children's hospital that would have dealt with this condition on a hundred other occasions. Jake was in good hands.

She picked up the item he'd flung at the wall. His wallet. It must have been the closest thing he'd had to hand. It fell open in her hands.

There, under a clear bit of plastic, was an old photograph. Two young children and a baby.

It wasn't quite old enough to be a black and white photo, but the colours had faded with age. The little girl's dress had probably been a vibrant pink. Now it was a paler version, her hair in dark curls about her shoulders. The boy was barely an inch taller than her, his dark hair and eyes unmistakeable.

But what made her stomach clench was the pride in their faces as they held their baby brother between them. The innocence of child-hood. The joy of family, as they held him on their knees.

Dante. This was Dante.

The tears welled up her eyes.

She sensed him next to her. His finger ran across the battered plastic.

'It's a lovely photograph,' she whispered.

He took the wallet from her hand. 'Yes, yes, it is.' He closed it tightly and slipped it into his back pocket.

There was hesitation, as if he was about to say something. What should she do? Should she wrap her arms around him?

He seemed so closed. So self-contained. She wanted to reach out but couldn't bear the thought of him brushing her aside. Maybe he needed time. Maybe he needed a little space.

Yes, that was it.

She should give him a little time to process what had just happened. It must be so hard for him. It must have dredged up a whole host of difficult memories.

The aspect of feeling out of control must have been the most terrifying of all.

And she could relate. Because it was exactly how she'd felt about her father.

He was still watching her. The tension crackled in the air.

If only she could take that step.

If only she could cross the treatment room and put her arms around him.

But something was stopping her. Something was gluing her feet to the floor and her arms at her sides.

He hesitated. 'We need to discuss this case at the next staff meeting and review the drugs we have available.' He nodded and turned and swept out the door.

Leaving Francesca rooted to the spot.

The feeling of regret swept over her like an icy chill.

It was the last time he was alone with her for three days.

CHAPTER TWELVE

GABRIEL looked furious.

And no wonder.

There, right in front of her, was the headline: *'Millionaire Doc Saves Drowning Teenager in Venice.'*

Her eyes swept over the newspaper thrust in front of her, a British tabloid that was prone to running scandalous stories of all descriptions.

And as she read the words her heart sank like a stone.

Gorgeous Doc Gabriel Russo, thirty-one, heir to the Russo Printing fortune, saved the life of a British teenager the other day after he fell into the harbour at Venice and was swept out to sea.

Eyewitnesses reported that Gabriel didn't hesitate and dived straight in, swimming to the teenager and making several attempts to bring him to the surface. Unfortunately he then had to be rescued himself as they were swept by the tide into the harbour wall and the Italian millionaire was knocked out.

He was resuscitated by British nurse Francesca Cruz, who serves on the same cruise ship as him.

Ryan Hargreaves, age thirteen, from Sussex, on holiday with his parents and younger sister, was successfully treated on board and managed to enjoy the rest of their holiday despite his ordeal. He is now safely at home.

Dr Russo had been working as a paediatrician in the States but recently came home to help out the family business after his father's health failed.

His skills haven't been wasted on the Italian cruise liner Silver Whisper, *as he's reportedly saved the life of another child, diagnosing an unusual case that, if missed, could have resulted in the child's death.*

The accompanying photo made her heart turn to ice. It was the snapshot she'd sent to Jill, showing Gabriel dressed in his white uniform, directing the ship-to-ship transfer of a patient during a routine crew exercise.

Some of the words in the newspaper article were copied almost directly from her email. Why on earth had Jill done this?

Her brain was scrambled. She'd known that Gabriel had refused any publicity about the incident. She just hadn't exactly known why.

'How could you?' he hissed, before slamming the newspaper down on the table in front of her. 'After everything that's happened between us. You sold confidential patient details, Francesca. The first rule for any health-care professional— never break patient confidentiality. That's the first thing any medical student learns.' The volume of his voice was increasing on a par with his rage. His face was becoming redder and redder. She'd seen his rage before with the dining-room manager and over the antibiotics and that had been scary enough. But this?

Her head was spiralling. She tried to speak, 'Gabriel, wait—'

'Did you really need the money so badly? Did you? How much did they pay you? How much was it worth to sell me out? Do you know what this will do to the family business? My father is the patriarch of the family. He's the figurehead that everyone expects to see. This will ruin him. Share prices will plummet once people know he's been unwell. You've just ruined a business that's been in my family for generations—all because of your greed!'

'Stop it!' She thudded her hand down on the desk as she pushed herself up from her chair. She couldn't listen to this a second longer. He thought she'd sold this story? He thought she'd do something like this? Betray patient confidentiality?

How dared he? Surely he knew her well enough to know that she would never do anything like this?

'Stop it now!' She picked up the newspaper in disgust. 'I'm not responsible for this, Gabriel. I would never do something like this.'

'So who is their source, then, Francesca? Because they know things that shouldn't have left this cruise ship. And how the hell did they get their hands on that picture?'

She cringed. There was no hiding this. There was no getting away from any of this.

'I knew it,' he muttered furiously. 'I should have known you were just like your friend.'

What did that mean? She felt a cold chill wash over her skin. He thought she was a liar. The one thing in her life that she'd never been guilty of.

She couldn't stand this. She had to get things out in the open. 'Now...' She took a deep breath. 'Some of this I *am* responsible for.'

She pointed at the front of the newspaper. 'It was Jill. At least, I'm assuming it was Jill. She emailed a few weeks ago and I replied. I told her about the rescue and how I resuscitated you. I also told her you'd saved another child's life. But I never, *never* revealed any patient details to her.' She shook her head fiercely. 'I would never do that. I don't know where they got Ryan's name from, but it certainly didn't come from me.'

Her fingers touched the paper. 'The picture, however, did come from me. She asked me what you looked like these days. And I sent it to her.' She lifted her eyes to meet his. 'And for that I'm truly sorry.'

She waited a few moments for them both to catch their breath.

'Now maybe you'll tell me what you meant

about "being the same" as my friend Jill.' Her hands were shaking but she kept the tremor from her voice. Tiny jigsaw pieces were slotting together in her head—and she didn't like the picture they were forming.

He was trembling—still furious with her. It would be so easy to turn around and walk away. To storm off and open the Australian visa that was in the top drawer of her bedside cabinet. Book a flight and head off into the sunset.

But she didn't want to do any of that. She had to be grown up. She had to accept responsibility that some of this was her fault. Not the patient details but the Gabriel details.

For a few weeks life with Gabriel had almost crept into that dreamlike realm. The happy, blissful place where everything was tinged with pink. A few days of stolen kisses and secret moments.

But that had been before they'd looked after Jake. That had been before she'd seen his reaction to treating a child with meningitis.

Wearing rose-tinted glass was all very well but the reality check of life meant there would always be murky grey skirting around the edges.

And Francesca didn't want to walk away. Because for the first time in a long time she felt at home. At home with Gabriel.

It didn't matter that they were roaming the ocean on a cruise ship with no fixed abode. She felt relaxed and happy with Gabriel. And up until a few seconds ago she'd thought he felt the same with her.

For Francesca it was a revelation. It was the people that made the home, not the place.

She wanted to see this through. No matter where it would take her. She'd connected with him in a way she'd never experienced before and she wasn't about to let this slip through her fingers.

This was worth fighting for.

She took a deep breath. 'Tell me about Jill.'

His hands were fixed on the side of the desk, his knuckles white. His eyes met hers, his dark brown eyes almost black.

'Your friend is a thief. I threw her out when I discovered her hiding my watch in her bag. A few other things had gone missing and I'd had my suspicions. But this time I caught her—and her feet didn't touch the floor.'

She felt her throat close over. The hairs on her arms stood on end and an uneasy trickle crept down her spine.

There was no point in leaping to her defence. Jill had always been desperate for money. Francesca just hadn't known why. What's more, she hadn't *wanted* to know why.

'Do you know what, Gabriel? I'm sorry my friend did that. I have no idea why she did. It certainly wasn't anything that I knew about. But I have to be honest—to my knowledge, Jill never stole anything from me. Maybe I didn't have anything worth stealing. She was always diving from one get-rich-quick scheme to another but that didn't matter to me. What did matter was that when I really needed her, she was there for me. Just as I hope I will be for her. Particularly if she has problems.'

No one in life was perfect.

Not her. Not him. Not her father. And not Jill.

This was real life. Not some fairy-tale. Her father wasn't here to tell her those stories any more. He'd chosen a different path and it was time for Francesca to choose hers.

She reached her hand across the desk and touched Gabriel's cold skin.

Gabriel wasn't angry with her. He was angry at the set of circumstances he'd been dropped into. Things that were out of his control.

And she knew what that felt like.

Because she'd been there.

And so had he.

And what she wanted to do right now was help him. To prove to the man that she loved that she would stand by him through thick and thin.

She knew nothing about share prices. She didn't care about his money. Money had never been a factor in this relationship.

But what she did know was how it felt to have a family member to worry about. To want to ease the pressure and strain on them.

His hands were starting to loosen at the edge of the desk and she intertwined her warm fingers with his cool ones.

Hurt and confusion was written all over his face. And panic at the potential threat to his father's health and the family business.

This was it. This was the time to choose—between the dream job or the dream man. And she didn't hesitate.

'What can I do to help, Gabriel? Because I'm here for you. I'm not going anywhere.' She held his gaze and lifted his hand to her heart.

Gabriel was trying to control the anger he was feeling. Even as he'd shouted some of those words at Francesca he'd known couldn't be true.

Francesca could never be like Jill. The person he'd got to know over the last few weeks was warm and loving, not cold and desperate like her friend had been.

This was the woman who'd bared her soul to him and sobbed her heart out over her father's suicide.

She was one of the few people in his life he'd ever told about Dante. And he'd shared with her because he trusted her. Francesca Cruz was a good person. An honest person.

Even now, when he'd told her about Jill, she hadn't been reactive and angry. She'd immediately had some perspective and been rational about it.

He had to ask. He had to ask now. 'What are you running from, Francesca?'

He heard her sharp intake of breath.

'You've drifted from job to job, place to place. You hardly stay anywhere longer than six months. Hardly enough time to make friends— hardly enough time to get to know people. I heard that your next step will be Australia. When do you plan on going there? When do you plan on leaving?'

His head was swimming with how he felt about her. How he felt about everything. How he felt about his family.

'I'm not running, Gabriel,' she whispered as she tried to blink back tears. 'I'm just trying to find a place to call home.'

And it escaped. One single fat tear sliding down her perfect cheek.

But what would happen now? It would take the Italian press less than a few hours to pick up on the implication about his father's health.

Then it would be everywhere. He cringed. He had to get back home. He had to be with his family.

He'd come back to Venice to be near and to

help his family, not to hinder it. There had to be a way to put this right.

'I need to go. I need to leave.'

He could see the expression on her face, the quiet determination masking the hurt in her eyes.

To him, she'd never looked so beautiful.

The next few days would be a nightmare.

And, as much as he wanted to, he couldn't possibly lead her into that.

It wouldn't be fair. They'd only really just met. They'd only spent one precious night together. He couldn't possibly ask her to…

'Just give me time to pack.'

He blinked. And in that moment he knew.

The person he'd always been looking for was standing right in front of him. She was prepared to come and walk into the lion's den with him— right by his side. Francesca had been searching for home.

And it was the one thing he could give her.

The words clogged in his throat. 'Are you sure?'

She looked as though she might cry again. Maybe she wasn't sure. Maybe she just wanted to walk away.

He looked across at the deep brown eyes as she tilted her chin up towards him. If he was lucky, it would be the face he'd spend the next fifty years looking at. A force to be reckoned with.

'I've never been surer.'

EPILOGUE

EVERYTHING passed in a blur. A quick trip back to Venice followed by four more trips around the Med to see out their notice.

A press officer to deal with media enquiries.

A quiet phone call to a tearful friend who admitted she needed some help.

Gabriel's sister announced as the new, entirely capable CEO of the company.

Francesca fingered the still unopened envelope in her hand.

Australia. Her dream job—at least, that's what she'd thought.

She still hadn't told him—and she probably never would. Because everything she'd been looking for she'd found here, with him.

'What's your favourite fairy-tale?'

She smiled as she felt the warm breath at the back of her neck and his arms steal around her waist. She leaned back against his warm body, looking over at the city of Venice.

It was twilight and the twinkling scattered lights bobbed up and down on the inky-dark waters. Gabriel's penthouse with its gothic façade sat on the Misericordia canal. It was surrounded by gorgeous buildings and a fourteenth-century palace. Every girl's modern-day fairy-tale, with the gondolas slipping silently by at night. A perfect setting.

She sighed. 'I like a little bit from each of them. Snow White being kissed by the prince. Prince Charming sliding the shoe onto Cinderella's foot. Rapunzel throwing down her hair, and Sleeping Beauty being woken by a tender kiss.'

He smiled, showing his perfect white teeth. She turned around, her arms reaching up and twining around his neck.

This was her Gabriel. The tiny lines, caused by the worry and stress of the last few weeks, were dissipating. The tension was gone from his back and shoulders.

'You called me Sleeping Beauty once before.' She pulled back in surprise. 'You remember?

I thought you wouldn't remember any of that. Why didn't you tell me?'

He raised an eyebrow at her. 'And spoil all our fun?' He whispered in her ear. 'Do you know which part of the fairy-tales I like best?'

She shook her head.

'The happy ever after. Everyone deserves one of those.'

She felt herself freeze. The cool evening air danced over her skin, sending the hairs on her arms standing on end. Her breath caught in her throat.

It was just a moment because Gabriel had dropped to one knee and was holding a black velvet box out towards her.

His eyes were staring earnestly at her. 'Francesca Cruz, will you do me the honour of becoming my wife? In sickness and in health, through good times and bad, from here until the end of time? Because I've found my own fairy-tale, here, with you. And I can't imagine spending the rest of my life with anyone other than you.'

She couldn't speak. The words just wouldn't form.

It was perfect. Her own personal fairy-tale

with her own perfect hero. Her mum and dad would have loved him. Of that, she had no doubt. Just as Gabriel's family had welcomed her with open arms, making her feel instantly at home.

He opened the box and she blinked. Then smiled.

He stood up and slipped the ring from the box. 'You know that money was no object. You know I could have bought the biggest diamond in the world. But I wanted to buy something that was about us. Something about where we met.'

The ring was flawless. An exquisite aquamarine—the colour of the Mediterranean Sea—surrounded by a host of sparkling diamonds.

'It's perfect,' she breathed.

'Is that a yes?'

'Yes!' she screamed as she jumped up on him. 'Yes, yes, yes!' She smothered him in kisses as he laughed and held her tightly.

Her feet touched the floor again as he took a second to slide the ring onto her finger.

A wicked gleam crossed her eyes. 'It's not just fairy-tales I like,' she said.

'What do you mean?'

'Do you remember what I was reading on the boat?'

He remembered instantly, blood flushing through his heated skin. 'I remember,' he said slowly.

'Then I think it's time to act out my favourite part.'

And she held her hand out to him and led him to the bedroom.

* * * * *

Mills & Boon® Large Print
Medical

September

NYC ANGELS: REDEEMING THE PLAYBOY — Carol Marinelli
NYC ANGELS: HEIRESS'S BABY SCANDAL — Janice Lynn
ST PIRAN'S: THE WEDDING! — Alison Roberts
SYDNEY HARBOUR HOSPITAL: EVIE'S BOMBSHELL — Amy Andrews
THE PRINCE WHO CHARMED HER — Fiona McArthur
HIS HIDDEN AMERICAN BEAUTY — Connie Cox

October

NYC ANGELS: UNMASKING DR SERIOUS — Laura Iding
NYC ANGELS: THE WALLFLOWER'S SECRET — Susan Carlisle
CINDERELLA OF HARLEY STREET — Anne Fraser
YOU, ME AND A FAMILY — Sue MacKay
THEIR MOST FORBIDDEN FLING — Melanie Milburne
THE LAST DOCTOR SHE SHOULD EVER DATE — Louisa George

November

NYC ANGELS: FLIRTING WITH DANGER — Tina Beckett
NYC ANGELS: TEMPTING NURSE SCARLET — Wendy S. Marcus
ONE LIFE CHANGING MOMENT — Lucy Clark
P.S. YOU'RE A DADDY! — Dianne Drake
RETURN OF THE REBEL DOCTOR — Joanna Neil
ONE BABY STEP AT A TIME — Meredith Webber

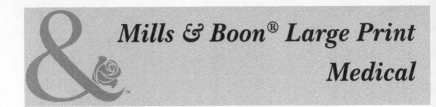

Mills & Boon® Large Print

Medical

December

NYC ANGELS: MAKING THE SURGEON SMILE	Lynne Marshall
NYC ANGELS: AN EXPLOSIVE REUNION	Alison Roberts
THE SECRET IN HIS HEART	Caroline Anderson
THE ER'S NEWEST DAD	Janice Lynn
ONE NIGHT SHE WOULD NEVER FORGET	Amy Andrews
WHEN THE CAMERAS STOP ROLLING...	Connie Cox

January

DR DARK AND FAR-TOO DELICIOUS	Carol Marinelli
SECRETS OF A CAREER GIRL	Carol Marinelli
THE GIFT OF A CHILD	Sue MacKay
HOW TO RESIST A HEARTBREAKER	Louisa George
A DATE WITH THE ICE PRINCESS	Kate Hardy
THE REBEL WHO LOVED HER	Jennifer Taylor

February

MIRACLE ON KAIMOTU ISLAND	Marion Lennox
ALWAYS THE HERO	Alison Roberts
THE MAVERICK DOCTOR AND MISS PRIM	Scarlet Wilson
ABOUT THAT NIGHT...	Scarlet Wilson
DARING TO DATE DR CELEBRITY	Emily Forbes
RESISTING THE NEW DOC IN TOWN	Lucy Clark

0813 LP 2P P2